Detour for Romance

Tim picked up Nikki's book bag and slung it over his shoulder. "I'll walk you to the parking lot," he said.

"You can do better than that," Nikki said lightly, tossing her key ring to him. "I thought maybe you'd like to drive me home."

Tim glanced toward Nikki's gleaming, metallic blue Camaro. "No thanks," he said, tossing the keys back to her. "Maybe some other time, okay?" Turning quickly, he dashed across the lot to his mother's car and drove off without even glancing back.

Nikki was stunned. What was going on? Tim had acted so cold and distant. There had to be more to Tim's phobia about her car than simple pride or envy.

There was something else, something Tim Cooper didn't want her to know about.

RIVER
HEIGHTS

#2

GUILTY
SECRETS

CAROLYN
KEENE

AN ARCHWAY PAPERBACK
Published by POCKET BOOKS
New York   London   Toronto   Sydney   Tokyo

AN ARCHWAY PAPERBACK *Original*

An Archway Paperback published by
POCKET BOOKS, a division of Simon & Schuster Inc.
1230 Avenue of the Americas, New York, NY 10020

ISBN: 0-671-67760-8

First Archway Paperback printing November 1989

10 9 8 7 6 5 4 3 2 1

AN ARCHWAY PAPERBACK and colophon are
registered trademarks of Simon & Schuster Inc.

RIVER HEIGHTS is a trademark of Simon & Schuster Inc.

Printed in the U.S.A.

IL 6+

 **1**

Nikki Masters whipped the lens cap off her camera. "Smile and say 'Bash the Bears,'" she called, focusing on Lacey Dupree.

"Oh, Nikki, no!" Lacey wailed. "Not now!" She was precariously balanced on top of a stepladder, trying to tape up a nine-foot-long poster in a hallway of River Heights High North.

The dismissal bell clanged. Students spilled out of the classrooms, and the hallways came alive with laughter and excited chatter.

Lacey clung to the ladder as Nikki snapped several shots.

"Not funny, Masters," Lacey called down. "Not funny at all!" But she grinned as she pounded a piece of tape against the wall with her fist. Then she stepped down one rung and leaned back to survey her efforts.

Nikki studied the blue-and-white football poster, a cartoon of a River Heights Raider poised over a cowering Bedford High Bear. "It looks great. Hey, can you see Robin from up there?"

Lacey scanned the teeming hallway. "Not yet."

Robin Fisher and Lacey Dupree had been Nikki's best friends forever. The two girls were as unlike as day and night, but red-haired, romantic Lacey and dark, practical Robin had always been there for Nikki.

Suddenly Lacey pointed over several bobbing heads. "There's Robin now—with Calvin, of course. Between the swim team and Calvin, she doesn't have much time for us anymore."

"Give her a break," Nikki said. "She's in love."

Lacey waved frantically, trying to catch Robin's attention. "Over here! Hey, Fisher!"

Nikki watched as Calvin Roth gave Robin a quick kiss on the cheek. He waved to Lacey, then headed off in the opposite direction.

Robin blushed, catching Lacey's gaze. "See ya later," she called over her shoulder to

Calvin, and began to thread her way through the crowd.

"Look out, Fisher!" Lacey cried as Robin ducked under her ladder. "Don't you know it's bad luck to walk under a ladder?"

Nikki clicked off a shot of Robin.

"Oh, come on, Lace," Robin said, stepping out from her ladder cage. "You don't believe all that superstitious stuff, do you?" Dressed in a black miniskirt and a long turquoise T-shirt cinched with a black belt, Robin was her usual stylish self. She pointed at Nikki's camera. "Are the pictures for the school paper?"

Nikki nodded, and Lacey groaned.

Nikki glanced at the ladder. "Hey, watch where you're going—"

It was too late. Jeremy Pratt, River Heights High's super snob, slammed his shoulder into the ladder. It wobbled crazily. Lacey shrieked and grabbed the top step to keep her balance.

Just as the ladder was about to topple, Jeremy righted it. "Don't you know this thing's a hazard? Some people have no respect for student safety."

Nikki stepped forward. "Maybe you should be more careful."

Jeremy's green eyes narrowed on Nikki.

"I'll remember that. I have a great memory, Nikki," he said, then sauntered off.

"What was that all about?" Lacey asked as she climbed down from her unsteady perch.

Nikki shook her head. "I guess he's still mad."

Robin's smile grew. "You mean because of what you did to him at Commotion last week?"

"Probably," Nikki replied. Nikki had chosen to dance with someone other than Jeremy at Commotion. "But let's not worry about Jeremy. How about if we meet at Strawberry's for a soda after I'm through with play practice and Robin gets done swimming?"

Robin shrugged. "None of us has wheels, remember?"

"We can probably get a ride with someone," Nikki said.

Lacey adjusted the waistband of her long denim skirt and shook her head. "Sorry, I can't. I've got to work at the record shop until the mall closes."

"And I'm going to study with Calvin after swim practice," Robin said happily. "Maybe you and Tim should go."

Nikki nodded. She and Tim Cooper had

been dating only a very short time, but already she was crazy about him.

Lacey snapped the ladder shut and walked it over to the custodian's closet. After she shoved it in, she wagged a finger at Nikki. "Don't you dare give those pictures to DeeDee until I see them first!"

Nikki laughed. DeeDee Smith was editor of the school paper. "You know, if these shots are good enough, they might even make the yearbook!"

Lacey glanced at her watch. "Listen, I've got to take off pretty soon. I'm scheduled to be in the record store every night from now until homecoming. Some of us," she added good-naturedly, *"do* have to work for a living, you know."

Nikki cringed just a little, even though she knew Lacey was only teasing. The Masters family's wealth was hardly a secret, after all. "And as for our transportation problem," Lacey went on, smiling as she studied her nails, "I may have it solved."

"How?" Robin asked.

"I'm going to buy a car," Lacey announced.

"You are?" Nikki cried. "That's great!"

Robin perked up. "When?"

Lacey grinned. "As soon as I save the money!"

"Oh." Robin looked disappointed. "I guess I won't hold my breath."

"Maybe we shouldn't give up hope entirely," Nikki said.

Robin's eyebrows shot up. "Why not?"

"Because my dad is finally giving in."

"He's buying you a car?" Robin said, whooping in delight. "This is *too* much!"

"I know," Nikki said. "I can't believe it, either. At least, not until I'm actually behind the wheel. That's why I haven't said anything—just in case my dad changes his mind."

"He wouldn't, would he?" Lacey asked anxiously.

"I don't think so, but"—Nikki lowered her voice an octave in a poor imitation of her dad—"'You know, Nikki, I didn't have a car until I was in college.'"

Lacey giggled as Nikki added, "But Grandpa told him that times have changed. He's really been on Dad's case."

"And your dad still said 'no way,'" Robin guessed.

Nikki nodded. "But that was months ago. Grandpa's been working on him, and I think my dad has finally changed his mind"—she deepened her voice again—"'*If* you get a practical vehicle. No flashy sports car!'"

"Who cares if it's practical?" Lacey said. "As long as it has four wheels and moves!"

"Right," Robin agreed, smiling at Nikki. "Though I don't have to find rides after practice anymore. Calvin's been driving me home every night."

Nikki grinned. "Just how serious is this relationship?"

Robin laughed. "Serious enough, I guess."

"You're with that guy all the time—" Lacey began.

Nikki gave her a nudge with her elbow. "It's okay," Nikki said. "We're glad you're in love. Aren't we, Lacey?"

"Sure," Lacey said, shooting Nikki a dirty look.

"So, tell us everything," Nikki prodded.

A dazzling smile spread across Robin's face. "What can I say? Cal's the greatest! I can't imagine life without him. Everything's going great—uh-oh!" She had caught a glimpse of Nikki's watch. "Look, I've got to run. The coach'll kill me if I'm late again." Robin took off down the hall, the heels of her flats slapping against the floor.

Lacey bit her lower lip. "You know, Nikki, I'm happy for Robin, I really am. But I can't help being a little worried about her, too."

Nikki frowned. "Worried? Why?"

"She's never been hung up on a guy before." Lacey's pretty brow puckered thoughtfully as they walked down the hall.

"Oh, lighten up, Lace," Nikki said. "Isn't it great that Robin is finally in love?"

"Yes," Lacey said, "but Robin isn't herself. All she ever thinks about is Calvin."

"And sports," Nikki reminded her as they reached Nikki's locker. "And school. And us." Nikki twirled the combination lock, and the door swung open, revealing the glossy black-and-white picture she'd taken of Tim the week before. Nikki glanced at the photo and smiled to herself.

She placed her camera on the top shelf and grabbed her script of *Our Town,* the play in which she'd won the lead role of Emily. Tim had landed the romantic lead opposite her, and Nikki couldn't have been happier.

"Are you coming or what?" Lacey asked, startling Nikki from her daydreams of Tim.

"Sure." Swinging her jean jacket over one shoulder, Nikki slammed her locker door shut.

"Nikki! Nikki Masters!" Cheryl Worth, the student council president, was half running toward them. Her light brown hair bobbed to the tempo of her quick footsteps, and she was waving one arm frantically. Nancy Drew was right behind her. What, Nikki wondered, was Nancy doing at school?

Nancy, a famous amateur detective and one of her friends, lived next door to Nikki. Only a short time earlier Nancy had helped prove Nikki innocent in a murder investigation.

"What're you doing here?" Nikki teased Nancy as she and Cheryl came up.

Nancy laughed. "Actually, I was looking for you."

"Uh-oh," Lacey said, her blue eyes growing round. "Don't tell us—a crime has been committed right here in the hallowed halls of River Heights High."

"Hardly," Nancy said with a grin. "I just had a meeting about homecoming."

"Nancy's heading the alumni committee for the halftime show at the game this year," Cheryl added.

"That's terrific, Nan!" Nikki said.

The River Heights homecoming football game always attracted a large crowd, and each year several recent graduates put on a skit at halftime. Nancy would do a great job, Nikki knew.

Nancy's smile widened. "And that's not all the news. Guess who we just chose as student coordinator?" She looked straight at Nikki.

"Me?" Nikki asked in surprise.

Nancy grinned. "You bet. Congratulations."

Nikki could hardly believe her good luck. Being chosen student coordinator for the alumni skit was quite an honor.

"So what do you say?" Nancy asked.

"You'll do it, won't you?" Cheryl prodded.

"I-I'd love to!" Nikki replied.

"Oh, Nik, this is *sooo* great!" Lacey said, hugging her friend.

"When's the next meeting?" Nikki asked.

"Tomorrow at my house," Nancy replied. "Seven P.M. sharp. Be there!"

"I will," Nikki promised. Then she clapped a hand to her forehead. "Oh, no! I almost forgot. I've got to get to rehearsal. Everyone's probably waiting for me."

"Yeah, I'm out of here, too," Lacey said. "Minimum wage beckons."

Nikki turned just as Brittany Tate, the most popular, prettiest, and most scheming girl in the junior class, rounded the corner.

Inwardly, Nikki groaned. She didn't hate Brittany, not really, but she certainly didn't trust her. Brittany had almost succeeded in breaking Tim and her up, and so Nikki preferred to steer clear of her.

Brittany nearly tripped as she turned the corner. There, near Nikki Masters's locker, a small group had gathered. Brittany's mind began racing faster than her feet when she caught sight of Nancy Drew in the crowd. What was she doing at school? There was only one way to find out.

Brushing her long dark hair away from her big brown eyes, she headed toward Nikki's locker. "Nancy!" she said sweetly, ignoring the other girls. "What are you doing here? You're investigating a crime, right?"

Nancy laughed. "No. Sorry."

"Come on, you can let me in on it," Brittany said, the wheels beginning to turn in her mind. If she got a scoop, she could print it in the homecoming edition of "Off the Record," her column for the school newspaper, the *Record*.

"Really," Nancy insisted. "I'm here only as an alumna."

Brittany's smile faded. She was getting a bad feeling about this.

"I'm on the alumni committee," Nancy said. "We just had a meeting in the library and elected Nikki as student coordinator for the alumni skit. I thought I'd personally tell her the good news before I left."

"You chose Nikki?" Brittany repeated, feeling as if she'd been kicked in the stomach. She'd thought *she* was a shoo-in for that spot. She'd already spent hours with Ben Newhouse, the junior class president, working on the halftime show. And she'd told everyone she would be alumni coordinator. What could she do?

"That's right," Nancy said, nodding. "She'll do a great job!"

"Of course she will," Brittany agreed, struggling to keep her cool. "Congratulations, Nikki."

"Thanks," Nikki replied simply.

"Well, I've got to run," Nancy said. "See you all soon!" With a friendly wave, she walked quickly toward the doors leading to the parking lot.

Brittany seethed silently. Burned and humiliated by Nikki again. She forced a smile, aware of Nikki scrutinizing her. "I guess we'll be working together, Nikki."

"Together?" Nikki raised her eyebrows.

Thinking fast, Brittany said, "Ben Newhouse asked for my help on the halftime show. I've already organized the floats and the band and—" Brittany felt a lump form in her throat. "Ben said I'd be student coordinator, but I guess they chose you instead. I'm going to have a talk with Ben about his telling little stories to get me to do his work."

Nikki felt rotten. Though she didn't trust Brittany, she didn't want to hurt her, either. Brittany was smart and pretty and, when she wanted to be, funny.

"I didn't know you were interested in being student coordinator," Nikki said.

"Oh, not really. It was just that Ben *said* I was. It doesn't matter," Brittany said with a shrug. "Well, we'll just have to work together to make it the best show ever."

Nikki wished she could believe Brittany. She seemed sincere. But she'd trusted Brittany before, and the girl had tried to turn Tim against her. No, Nikki decided, she definitely could not trust Brittany. At least, not yet.

Brittany managed a little smile, hoping it made her look kind of vulnerable. "Look, I know you probably don't want to work with me—"

"It's okay," Nikki said, feeling awful.

"Well, all that business with Tim—" Brittany hesitated. "It was a pretty lousy thing to do," she said, staring at her shoes, pretending she was unable to face Nikki.

Nikki said nothing.

Brittany blushed, embarrassed that her ploy hadn't worked, and cleared her throat. "Listen, Nikki, I'll talk to you later. I've got a column to write." Turning swiftly, she started down the hall.

Nikki felt about one inch tall. Holding a grudge was petty. "Hey, wait!" she called.

Brittany stopped and whirled around.

"You're right," Nikki said, catching up to Brittany. "Maybe we should start over."

Brittany shifted her huge brown eyes around the hall, then shrugged one slim shoulder. "Okay. It's both our necks this time."

Nikki almost grinned. Brittany wasn't really interested in making up with her. She just wanted a little of the glory for herself.

"Look, I really am sorry about that mess with Tim," Brittany said. "But it wasn't my fault, not really—"

Nikki waved the apology away. "Ancient history," she said, feeling more than a little uneasy.

"Well, look, I've got to go," Brittany said. "See you later."

"Right," Nikki said. Now she was *really* late for rehearsal. As she headed for the auditorium, she shoved all thoughts of Brittany aside and started thinking about Tim again. Just picturing his handsome face with his slate gray eyes and dimpled smile brought goose bumps to her skin and a smile to her lips. Her boyfriend was definitely the cutest boy at River Heights High!

And, she added to herself, the most mysterious. But she wasn't going to think about that now.

2 ～〜

Once Brittany was out of Nikki's sight, the smile dropped from her face. She clutched her books tightly. It wasn't fair! Why should Nikki be chosen student coordinator when she'd done nothing? She, Brittany, had done *everything* to get the halftime show on its feet!

Nikki Masters. No matter which way Brittany turned, she always came up against that girl's social position, her wealth, her charm. Nikki was cute, bright, and fun. With her sun-streaked blond hair, bright blue eyes, and quick, dimpled smile, Nikki had it all.

But Nikki wasn't the most popular girl in school. Brittany felt comforted by the fact that she herself was the girl with the most friends and the most dates. Why, she could have just about any boy at River Heights High! Everyone looked up to her, and everyone read her column in the *Record*. They had to, to keep up with the latest gossip.

"Hey, Brittany! Aren't you supposed to be in the newsroom?"

"What?" Brittany was startled and spoke sharply.

Kim Bishop, blond and trim, raced down the stairs toward her. Kim was one of Brittany's best friends. A large pink bag swung from Kim's shoulder, and she was still wearing a sweatband around her head. Obviously, Kim had just finished practicing with the dance team. Breathing heavily, Kim wiped a lingering drop of sweat from her forehead. "I thought you had a deadline this afternoon."

"I do." Brittany sighed.

"So why are you hanging around here?" Kim asked.

"I was just talking to Nikki Masters," Brittany replied.

Kim's blue eyes gleamed with interest. "Oh, yeah? What about?"

"Homecoming. We're going to be working on the halftime skit together." There was no point in mentioning that Nikki had been named the official alumni student coordinator, Brittany told herself.

"Lucky you," Kim said.

"Oh, I am," Brittany assured her. A plan to put Nikki in her place once and for all was just taking shape in her mind. "Just you wait and see."

Kim raised her eyebrows. "What's up?"

"I'll let you know later," Brittany promised, "but right now I've got to get moving. DeeDee's probably stomping around the office, waiting for my column."

Brittany started off down the hall again at a fast trot and hoped she could slip into the newsroom unnoticed.

After shoving open the *Record* office door, Brittany made her way quickly to a typewriter. When were they going to get computers? she wondered.

"Oh, Brittany! Did you hear?" Karen Jacobs called loudly. A junior who worked on layout and production, Karen was cute in an ordinary way, but she definitely needed lessons in how to put herself together. Her skirts were unflattering, her makeup nonexistent, and her hair usually pulled back in a boring clip. Karen was all business and not much fun.

"Hear what?" Brittany asked without interest. She tossed her purse onto the floor.

"Nancy Drew is going to be in charge of the alumni skit!"

Brittany rolled her eyes as she flopped into her chair. "I heard already."

"Isn't that great?" Karen said.

"If you say so," Brittany agreed, her voice tinged with sarcasm as she rolled a sheet of paper into her typewriter. She eyed Karen's messy work area and the huge stack of paperback murder mysteries near her In box. No wonder Karen thought Nancy Drew was such hot stuff, Brittany decided. She was addicted to mysteries.

"Well, if you ask me," said DeeDee Smith, catching Brittany's eye, "anything Nancy does is news with a capital *N.*"

"Like getting Nikki off the hook on that murder case, you mean?" Brittany asked innocently.

DeeDee and Karen exchanged a glance, and Brittany pretended not to notice. She had to keep her true feelings for Nikki under wraps. Otherwise the plan that was hatching in her mind would never work.

Karen cleared her throat nervously. "Well, as my father would say, what happened to Nikki is all water over the dam."

"Right," Brittany said, staring at her type-writer as if bored with the conversation.

DeeDee chewed on the end of her pen. "You know," she said slowly, "I think that we could really make something of this." Behind her glasses, DeeDee's brown eyes narrowed thoughtfully. "Brittany, I want you to interview some of the alumni who'll be in the halftime skit. You can do a special piece on them in your column."

"The alumni?" Brittany repeated. "Not for *this* issue?"

DeeDee nodded. "Yep, for this issue. You'll have only a couple of days. Deadline's Wednesday morning. We're doing a special homecoming issue on Friday instead of Monday next week."

"That's not enough time!" Brittany pro-tested.

"You can do it," DeeDee told her, and Brittany glowed with the praise in spite of herself.

"Dig through the files and microfiche and find out what the members of the alumni committee did while they were students here," DeeDee went on. "Check the year-book; find out what their classmates thought about them — you know, if they were chosen Most Likely to Succeed, that sort of thing.

Then find out what they're doing now. You only have to interview three or four people. That's all we'll have room for."

Picking up a pen, Brittany scratched some notes. "Then and Now," she whispered the tentative title almost to herself. The story did have some appeal.

"Talk to Nancy Drew, and get in touch with Claire Halliday, the jazz singer. She's on the committee, too, right?" DeeDee said.

Brittany nodded. She knew everyone on the alumni committee because of the work she'd already done on the halftime program. "We're still waiting for a couple of others to respond to the invitations," she said.

DeeDee paced between the desks. Brittany could almost see the wheels turning in her mind. "I think you should go to the next alumni meeting. Find out when it is and where. Someone must know."

Nikki Masters! Brittany frowned. "No problem," she said. "I'll be there."

Nikki sat on one end of the couch in a small room near the auditorium. The cushions of the worn sofa were lumpy, but she didn't mind. Nor did she care that the carpet was faded and the tables were littered with papers and used coffee cups. Old play programs and reviews were tacked to three large bulletin boards, and the afternoon sun filtered through partially drawn shades. But Nikki's attention was focused on Tim.

From the other end of the couch, Tim was staring at Nikki so hard that her throat ached. A wayward lock of dark hair fell over his forehead, and his expression was so intense that she couldn't look away. Though he was only playing a part, reading lines from *Our Town*, Nikki wondered if he meant the romantic things he was saying to her character.

"Nikki, that's your cue," he reminded her gently.

"What?" She glanced down at her script. "Oh, right." She closed her eyes for a moment, trying to concentrate on playing Emily, but her voice faded. The room seemed to grow smaller. Tim's gaze held hers, and Nikki remembered when he'd told her he loved her.

Now Tim was leaning forward, reaching for her hand. "You're the best thing that's ever happened to me. You know that, don't you?" he said, ignoring his script and letting it fall to the floor.

Nikki's heart somersaulted. She felt Tim's

hand warm on hers, and she could barely breathe.

The door suddenly banged open, and the custodian, whistling, pushed a huge plastic trash can into the room. He looked up, surprised to see Nikki and Tim. "Sorry, kids. I didn't know anyone was in here."

"It's okay," Nikki said quickly, feeling a blush climb up her neck.

Tim winked at her. "I guess we'd better get going," he said, his fingers slipping from her wrist.

"Right," Nikki replied breathlessly.

"Do you need a ride home?" Tim asked, smiling.

"That would be great!" Nikki picked up her purse and script, then followed Tim out of the room and into the deserted corridor.

The school was nearly empty; the only sounds were a few muted shouts echoing from the gym. Long banks of lockers lined both sides of the polished tile hallway, and huge homecoming posters decorated its walls.

Tim shouldered a side door open. Outside, the sun hung low in the cloudless sky. The air was crisp, and a fresh breeze rustled through the trees, snatching a few yellow leaves and scattering them on the lawn.

As they walked through the quad, Tim slung one arm over Nikki's shoulder and pulled her close. "I'm glad I found you," he said.

"Really?" Nikki looked up into his eyes.

"Uh-huh." Tim suddenly veered off the path, propelling Nikki behind a huge maple tree. Nikki giggled, but Tim's expression was serious. "When I moved here from Chicago last summer, I never thought I'd find a girl like you."

"Oh," Nikki whispered.

"You really are special, you know," he said, his eyes growing dark.

Nikki swallowed hard just as Tim's head moved closer and his lips brushed gently over hers.

A thrill swept down Nikki's body, and her knees buckled a little. She leaned against the rough bark of the old maple tree and felt the gentle pressure of Tim's mouth over hers. Her heart pumped crazily as her eyes closed.

"I'd better get you home," Tim said finally, reluctance heavy in his voice. "Come on."

Linking his fingers through Nikki's, he started to jog. She had to run to keep up with him. Her hair billowed away from her face, and she was almost out of breath by the time they reached the car.

Tim held the door for her. "Let's go down to the Loft."

"I'd love that," Nikki said happily as she slid into the passenger seat.

Tim drove slowly into town and parked in the lot behind the Loft, a fast-food restaurant that had once been an artist's studio. Lots of kids from River Heights High hung out there. Known for its exotic beverages, the Loft was one of Nikki's favorite spots.

Tim bought them each a milk shake at the counter. "No sane person drinks a raspberry marshmallow shake," he complained as he handed Nikki her pink drink and sat beside her in the booth.

Nikki grinned. "Try it. You might like it."

Tim made a face. "No, thanks. I think I'll stick to chocolate."

"Bor-ing, Cooper," Nikki said, but her smile faded as she spied Kim Bishop, Brittany Tate, and Samantha Daley entering the restaurant.

The three girls ordered and chose a table not far from Nikki and Tim's. Brittany waved and offered Nikki a quick smile before sitting down, but Kim and Samantha ignored her. Then Brittany plucked her compact from her purse and freshened her lipstick. The mirror glinted, and for a moment Nikki thought Brittany was watching her in the reflection.

"Nikki!"

Nikki turned and saw Robin and Calvin at the door. As Calvin went to the front to order, Robin slid into the booth across from Tim and Nikki.

"I thought you had to study," Nikki said.

Robin shrugged. "We got hungry."

Calvin brought a tray with two huge milk shakes, hamburgers, and french fries to the table. Robin grabbed a plate of fries, and the four of them talked about Calvin's latest science project. Calvin was a chemistry nut.

"Look, we really do have to study," Calvin said to Robin when they'd finished eating.

"I should be getting home, too," Tim agreed reluctantly.

They walked out to the parking lot, and Nikki watched as Robin climbed into Calvin's car. Calvin whispered something in her ear, and Robin giggled. There was no doubt about it, Nikki told herself. Robin was in love.

Tim took the long way to Nikki's house, and she snuggled close to him the whole time. The windows were rolled down, and the radio was playing a popular hit by the Deadbeats.

But Tim hardly glanced her way. His gaze was riveted on the road. Nikki couldn't help noticing how nervous he seemed. His hands clenched the wheel, and his mouth was set in a firm, narrow line.

What was wrong with him? Nikki wondered. He had seemed so happy at the Loft.

Tim drove through the gently curving streets and up the hill leading to the section of town where Nikki lived. Finally he turned left into the circular drive of the Masterses' home.

Nikki gazed at the house she'd lived in all her life. Though not nearly as grand as her grandfather's mansion, her house was beautiful. A three-story Tudor with a sharply pitched roof and steep gables, the stone and stucco house was surrounded by a velvet-green lawn. Flagstone paths led through well-tended gardens and curled around huge shade trees.

Nikki touched Tim's shoulder. "Can you come in for a minute?" she asked. "I can whip up some lemonade or iced tea. If we're lucky, there might even be some brownies."

"You're on, Masters," Tim said. But as she reached the door handle, he caught her in his arms and kissed her softly on the lips.

Nikki sighed happily. Her heart thudding

out of control, she moved closer to Tim and glanced at the rearview mirror. Her father was behind them! Quickly she pulled away from Tim. "We're not alone," she whispered as she opened the door and hopped out.

Tim, too, climbed out of the car.

"It's about time you showed up," Nikki's father said. Mr. Masters was tall, with thinning brown hair and a genuine smile. His eyes were as blue as Nikki's, and his face was tanned from hours of playing golf. His dog, a white-and-brown springer spaniel named Baltimore, bounded at his side. "Nikki, your grandfather has a surprise for you."

"Grandpa's here?" Nikki asked as Baltimore jumped up on her.

"Down, boy!" Mr. Masters commanded, but Baltimore ignored him.

Nikki patted the dog's head.

"Yes, your grandfather's here, around back near the garage," Mr. Masters replied, his eyes sparkling mysteriously. "And just for the record, I'm not sure I approve."

"Approve?" Nikki asked nervously. Of Tim?

"Go and see for yourself," Mr. Masters said.

"I will, right now. Oh, Dad, this is Tim Cooper. I don't think you've ever met him," Nikki said.

"Not officially," her father said.

As Mr. Masters shook Tim's hand, Baltimore bristled. Growling low in his throat, the dog's eyes never left Tim.

"Oh, stop it!" Nikki said with a laugh, turning to Tim. "Baltimore's bark is definitely worse than his bite."

"Your grandfather is waiting," Mr. Masters reminded her.

"Come on," Nikki told Tim, "I want you to meet Grandpa."

She led Tim around the corner of the house. Baltimore loped gamely at their heels, barking loudly, despite Mr. Masters's repeated commands.

Nikki stopped dead in her tracks as they reached the garage.

Her heart did a peculiar little flip. Her grandfather was waiting for her, all right. A distinguished-looking gray-haired man wearing a jaunty tweed cap, Mr. Masters, senior, was leaning against the fender of a shiny new Camaro with a T-roof! Its metallic blue paint dazzled Nikki. "Oh, Grandpa," she said, breathing out at the same time.

The elder Mr. Masters swung open the driver's door and motioned grandly toward it. "Happy birthday," he said with a wink.

Nikki's mouth dropped open. "But my birthday was months ago!"

Her grandfather chuckled. "I know, but your father is a very stubborn man. It took me all this time to convince him you needed a car."

"Stubborn, eh?" Nikki's father said, walking up to them.

The older man nodded. "Like a mule."

For a second Nikki couldn't speak. She'd known her father had relented, but she hadn't expected anything to happen so quickly. And the car! Never in her wildest dreams had she expected one like this.

"Well, don't you have anything to say?" her grandfather prodded.

"I love it!" Nikki dropped her books and ran forward to throw her arms around his neck. "Thank you, thank you, thank you! You're the absolute greatest!"

"Slow down now," the old man said, still smiling broadly. "There is a catch."

Nikki's soaring spirits did a nosedive. What could it be?

Her father cleared his throat and snapped a leash on Baltimore. "You may as well know

that I was not very happy about your grandfather's choice. I would have preferred something less flashy."

"Humph!" Mr. Masters, senior, interjected. "The car he wanted had no class at
all."

Nikki's father's lips were pinched in a
bloodless line. "But he insisted you have this
particular car. I agreed *only* if Grandpa
would let you pay for the gas and the upkeep
out of your allowance."

"I will!" Nikki cried, hardly believing her
good luck. She ran one finger along the sleek
hood, then climbed into the plush leather
seat and wrapped her fingers around the
steering wheel. Suddenly she spied Tim still
standing where she'd left him. Feeling a little
guilty for having forgotten him, she quickly
waved him over and climbed out of the car.
"Grandpa, I'd like you to meet Tim Cooper."

Her grandfather regarded Tim thoughtfully as they shook hands.

"Glad to meet you," Tim said, but his
handsome face seemed tense and a little
aloof.

"Why don't you take your young man for a
spin?" Nikki's grandfather suggested.

Nikki couldn't wait. "Climb in!" she said
to Tim, but he shook his head.

"Sorry. I can't. Not right now."

Nikki's mouth dropped open. "But—"

"I've really got to run, Nikki." Tim flashed her a quick smile, then turned and headed for the front of the house.

Nikki hesitated for a moment, then followed him. "Tim, wait!"

"I'll see you tomorrow," Tim called, climbing into his car.

Nikki couldn't believe he was leaving just like that. Swallowing hard, she turned back to the drive where her father and grandfather were standing near her new car.

"Strange fella," the elder Mr. Masters remarked when she rejoined them.

"He's really not," Nikki said, immediately jumping to Tim's defense, but she, too, thought his reaction to her new car was very odd. What had happened to him? One minute Tim was kissing her and the next he couldn't seem to get away fast enough!

"He'll get over it," her grandfather insisted, patting Nikki's shoulder as she slid the keys into the ignition. The powerful engine sparked to life.

I hope so, Nikki thought, remembering how romantic things had been with Tim in the rehearsal room and again in the car. I certainly hope so!

 3

After winding a rubber band around the end
of her French braid, Nikki stepped back from
the mirror and surveyed her reflection. She
added another dab of pink lip gloss and a
couple of swipes of mascara, then
straightened the hem of her white denim
miniskirt.

"Well, that's the best I can do," she said
aloud. She added silver hoop earrings, then
reached for the phone.

Lacey picked up on the second ring.

"Ready for school?" Nikki asked.

Lacey yawned. "Not really. I may miss the
bus today."

Nikki tried not to laugh. "The bus is on its
way."

"Of course it's on its way," Lacey said, sounding annoyed. "You called me up to say *that?*"

"Right. Hurry up and get ready!" Nikki said. "I'll see you in a few minutes!"

After hanging up the phone, Nikki went to the window. Through the glass, she could see the blue metallic sheen of her new Camaro glinting in the morning sunlight. An early frost powdered the lawn, and the last of her mother's chrysanthemums were beginning to wilt.

Sighing, Nikki remembered how strange Tim had acted yesterday. What was wrong with him?

She leaned one shoulder against the cool glass. She loved Tim, she was sure of it, but there were so many things she didn't know or understand about him. Sometimes she felt that he was intentionally shutting her out, even hiding something from her. But what?

That's silly, Nikki told herself. What could Tim possibly have to hide? Maybe he was just jealous because he didn't have a car of his own. But that didn't seem like Tim.

"Nikki! It's about that time!" Mrs. Masters called from the first floor.

"Coming!" Nikki slid into her flats,

snatched her book bag and purse, and hurried out of her bedroom.

Trailing one hand down the curved banister, Nikki made her way downstairs.

She pushed open the swinging doors to the kitchen and found her mother forking apple muffins onto a platter.

Mrs. Masters, a willowy woman with soft blond hair, green eyes, and a small, perfectly formed mouth, glanced at her daughter. "Excited?" she asked.

"About the car?" Nikki nodded. "It's amazing."

"I hope you thanked your grandfather."

"Over and over again!" Nikki swiped a warm muffin from the tray and plopped down at the table.

"I'll probably be in the studio when you get home," Mrs. Masters said as Nikki poured herself a glass of juice from the pitcher. "I'm trying to finish up Mrs. Donaldson's portrait." Mrs. Masters was an artist, and she worked long hours in a large, airy loft over the garage.

"I'll be late today, Mom," Nikki replied. "I have rehearsal."

"So I won't see you until dinner?" Mrs. Masters poured herself a cup of coffee and sat down at the table with Nikki. "I don't suppose you'll want to go out and just drive around?"

"Well . . ." Nikki's voice trailed away.

Mrs. Masters grinned. "Just be home by seven."

"I will," Nikki promised, finishing her muffin and gulping down the rest of her juice. She gave her mother a quick kiss, then sprinted out the door to her new car. She couldn't wait to see the looks on Lacey's and Robin's faces.

Lacey's mouth dropped open when Nikki stopped at the curb only a few minutes before the bus was due. "Is this *yours*? For real?"

"For real!" Nikki answered with a flourish of her hand.

"I can't believe it!" Lacey gasped. "How? When? Where? Tell me *everything!*"

Nikki grinned. "Get in and I will."

Lacey tossed her purse and books into the back seat, wrapped her long magenta skirt around her legs, and slid into the passenger seat. "This is absolute heaven," she said, smoothing her hair. That day it was pinned on top of her head, and loose curls brushed her freckle-dusted cheeks. "Does Robin know about this?"

"Not yet." Nikki slid the transmission into gear. As she began to explain how she had gotten the car, Nikki merged with the early morning traffic.

A few minutes later Nikki pulled the Camaro into the driveway of the Fishers' modern cedar-and-glass home. With a wink at Lacey, Nikki tapped on the horn.

The front door burst open, and Robin, her athletic bag slung over one shoulder, dashed down the steps. She stopped dead in her tracks at the sight of the car. She whistled softly. "What's this?"

"Nikki's grandfather picked it out," Lacey said, obviously enjoying her friend's speech-lessness. She leaned forward to let Robin squeeze into the back seat. That day Robin was wearing a purple jumpsuit with a wide silver belt and silver earrings.

"I wish *my* grandfather was such a nice guy," Robin murmured.

"Me, too. But I guess I'll have to buy my own car." Lacey flipped down the visor, studied her reflection in the mirror, and dabbed at her lipstick.

Nikki backed the car onto the street. "Maybe you'll get a raise at the record shop," she said hopefully.

"Fat chance. Len's so tight he squeaks."

Lacey flipped the visor back up, then shoved a cassette into the tape deck.

"This really is a terrific car," Robin said enthusiastically, leaning forward between the bucket seats. Her dark hair brushed her cheek. "Why didn't you tell me?"

"I didn't know myself until yesterday after school," Nikki explained. "I tried to call you last night."

"Oh." Robin smiled, her cheeks flushing. "I guess I was on the phone with Calvin."

"So what do you two talk about all the time?" Lacey asked.

Robin shrugged. "Just stuff."

"What kind of stuff?" Lacey pressed.

"Nothing special," Robin replied a little testily.

"You and Calvin really seem to be hitting it off," Nikki said quickly, remembering how happy they had looked at the Loft.

"I guess so," Robin said.

"You guess so?" Lacey twisted around in surprise. "Don't you know?"

Robin leaned back in her seat. Nikki exchanged a quick glance with Lacey. In the rearview mirror Nikki caught a brief glimpse of Robin chewing on a fingernail.

"Is something wrong?" Nikki asked, returning her attention to the road ahead.

"Nothing's wrong!" Robin snapped.

"You're sure?" Lacey said.

"Hey, what is this? The third degree?"

"Look," Nikki said, "if you don't want to talk about it——"

"There's nothing to talk about!" Robin said, blinking rapidly. "Okay, yesterday Cal and I had a fight after we left the Loft. He called last night and we made up. It was no big deal!"

"Okay, okay." Nikki tried to act unconcerned as she turned into the parking lot. Didn't she know from firsthand experience how hot and cold relationships could blow?

Robin tossed her hair out of her face and squared her shoulders. "Look, I'm sorry I yelled," she said as Nikki cut the engine. "I've got a lot on my mind. I've never been this serious about a boy before, and I've got a big geometry test today, and yesterday the swim coach chewed me out——"

"It's okay," Nikki assured her.

"Sure. We all have bad days," Lacey agreed. "And boys do cause problems."

"Do they ever," Nikki said. Quickly she told her friends about Tim's odd behavior the day before. "One minute he was wonderful, and the next he couldn't get away from me fast enough!" Nikki sighed, feeling worried as she got out of the car. She had hoped that Tim would call the night before to explain his odd behavior, but the phone hadn't rung.

"Maybe he's just envious of you because of your new car," Lacey suggested, closing the passenger door behind her.

"I thought about that possibility," Nikki admitted, "but I don't think so. Tim isn't like that."

"You know, some guys feel weird when a girl drives them around," Robin offered. "He doesn't have his own car, does he?"

"No, but he does get to use his mom's," Nikki answered.

"There you go," Robin said triumphantly.

"Robin's right. Maybe you should let him drive," Lacey said.

Nikki grinned. "I guess I should have thought of that myself."

By now a crowd had begun to gather around Nikki's new car. Robin spotted Calvin and waved. "See you later, you guys," she said. "And thanks for the ride, Nik."

Before Nikki could reply, Robin pushed her way through the crowd to Calvin. His green eyes lit up as he watched Robin moving toward him. A slow smile spread across his face, and as Robin reached him, he wrapped an arm around her waist and gave her a long kiss right in the middle of the parking lot.

Nikki looked away quickly.

Lacey's mouth dropped open. "Did you see *that?*" she whispered.

"I think the whole school did," Nikki replied.

Leaning against the railing near the door to the school's south wing, Brittany flipped through the latest copy of *Fashion Trends*. The willowy models all had wide smiles and sexy gazes, but Brittany was able to find fault with each one.

"I wonder who does her makeup?" she said to Kim, pointing to a red-haired model dressed in a wool cape and leather boots. "Elvira?"

"Or the Wicked Witch of the West," Kim said snidely, tossing her long blond hair. "B.A.D." Suddenly she froze. "I don't believe it!"

Brittany followed Kim's gaze. She squinted against the morning glare glancing off the hoods of cars in the parking lot, then nearly dropped her magazine.

"Do you suppose that's Nikki's new car?" Kim asked, astonished.

Brittany's heart plummeted. The Camaro

was the most beautiful car she'd ever seen! It *couldn't* be Nikki's! "I thought her father wouldn't let her have a car," she said finally.

Kim sighed. "Well, he must have changed his mind."

In despair, Brittany watched as a crowd gathered around the metallic blue Camaro, the very car of her own dreams. But she couldn't possibly afford it. A familiar lump filled Brittany's throat. Why? she wondered, forcing back tears of envy. Why did Nikki get everything she wanted? First Tim Cooper and now this!

Brittany withered a little inside when she remembered that her own father had given her a car not long ago. Little more than a pile of junk, the wretched car had died a painful death right in this very parking lot. Fortunately, no one had ever found out that the miserable wreck was hers—except the person who blackmailed her into confessing to Tim that she had tried to break him and Nikki up. She didn't know who the blackmailer was, but it was probably Robin Fisher or that mouse Lacey Dupree.

"Are you okay?" Kim asked.

Brittany realized that her fists were clenched and she had crumpled her magazine. "I'm fine," she said evenly. "What happens to Nikki Masters doesn't concern me."

Kim laughed harshly. "Since when?"

"I'm a bigger person than she is," Brittany said with a shrug.

"Oh, right." Kim nodded. "You aren't concerned in the least that Nikki's father owns the company your dad works for. And it doesn't bother you that she ended up with Tim Cooper. And now you couldn't care less that she has the most gorgeous car that's ever rolled into the River Heights parking lot."

Brittany bit her tongue. Kim knew just how to needle her, but she wasn't going to let Kim see how much it hurt. "I said it really doesn't matter."

Kim smiled sweetly. "I believe you. Even though you *were* watching Nikki and Tim in your mirror yesterday at the Loft."

"I was only checking out the competition," Brittany said just as sweetly.

The first bell clanged loudly, and Kim headed into the building.

Brittany didn't move. She stood for a few moments, staring at the beautiful car. She wanted to die.

Maybe you should go ahead with your plan, a small voice inside her head nagged. Show Nikki Masters up once and for all.

Brittany shuddered. The last time she'd tried to trick Nikki, the plan had backfired, with disastrous results. But maybe this could be a foolproof way to give Nikki a taste of humiliation.

"Don't do it!" Brittany startled herself by speaking out loud. But her scheme was beginning to have a life of its own. This time, Brittany told herself, she'd be careful. *Very* careful. And it would all be worth it!

 **4**

Nikki's stomach churned nervously as she slid into her seat in homeroom. She glanced over at Tim's desk—empty.

Was he ever going to show up? Nikki began to tap her pale pink nails on her desk.

As the classroom began to fill up, Nikki kept her eyes glued to the door. Would Tim be himself, or would he be secretive and strange, as he had been for no apparent reason the day before?

She spotted him the minute he entered the room, and her heart lurched at the sight of him. Tim's gray eyes found hers, and he smiled slightly. As he passed her desk, he slipped a note onto her stack of books.

Nikki looked at him curiously as he took

his seat and then opened the little square of paper. It simply said, "I love you."

Nikki recreased the note on the original fold lines. Tim wasn't angry with her! She openly looked at him, and he flashed her his irrepressible smile. How could she have ever doubted him? Her throat felt tight as she slipped the precious note into her purse.

The second bell rang just as Mrs. Sheedy, a short, sturdy woman dressed in a brown tweed suit and sensible shoes, took her place in front of the class. "Okay, now, listen up. We have a few announcements this morning." She peered at her students over the tops of her reading glasses. "First things first. Several locker thefts have been reported. If you know of anyone . . ."

Mrs. Sheedy droned on for the next few minutes, but Nikki barely heard a word. She was so wrapped up in her own happiness that she couldn't have cared less about locker thefts, the lunch menu, or school activities. Not that day.

When homeroom was finally dismissed, Nikki began to gather her books and suddenly felt Tim's strong arm around her waist. "I'll walk you to your next class," he said.

When she got to class, Nikki could barely concentrate. Her next class dragged as well, and Nikki kept her eye on the clock, springing from her chair at the exact second the dismissal bell rang.

She ran to her locker and found Tim standing there, grinning at her. "Hey, Emily, how about a hamburger after rehearsal today?"

Nikki laughed. "Sure, George," she teased, "as long as it's not at Mr. Morgan's drugstore in *Our Town.*"

Tim smiled and held up a palm. "I promise. No strawberry phosphates. Just a hamburger and fries."

"Then I wouldn't miss it for the world," Nikki said.

"Good, it's a date." Tim watched as Nikki picked up her book of Shakespeare's tragedies. "Ready for McNeil?" he asked.

"As ready as I'll ever be." Mr. McNeil was their honors English teacher. He was young and gawky-looking with oversize features, but he was one of the best teachers at River Heights. Mr. McNeil commanded respect in his classroom.

"I don't suppose you've read *Macbeth?*" Tim asked.

"The first two acts." Nikki slammed her locker shut. "Have you?" she asked him as they headed upstairs to room 209.

Tim shook his head. "Nah. I was too busy studying my lines last night." Tim shoved one hand into the pocket of his jeans as they reached the door.

"What if he gives us a pop quiz?" Nikki asked.

Tim laughed. "I don't have to worry. I was in a production of *Macbeth* last year in Chicago." He grinned. "Go ahead. Ask me anything about *Macbeth*."

"I don't think I know enough to come up with even one sensible question," Nikki told him. "Besides, I believe you."

"Good." Tim opened the classroom door just as the final bell rang.

Nikki quickly settled into her seat and turned around to grin at Tim across the room. She was rewarded with a heart-stopping smile. She dropped her eyes and opened her book. Why, she wondered, had she ever doubted how he felt about her?

"Okay, that should do it!" Mrs. Burns, the petite drama coach, told the cast of *Our Town*. Short and wiry, with springy brown hair, an upturned nose, and enthusiasm that infected everyone, Mrs. Burns was standing on the apron of the stage. The cast lounged in the first few rows of seats. "Rehearsal tomorrow after school. After that, we won't meet again until next week," Mrs. Burns went on. "Tomorrow we'll do a read-through, but next week I expect all of you to know your lines. Starting next Tuesday, we'll finish up blocking. Any questions?"

No one raised a hand.

"That's it, then, people," Mrs. Burns said. "See you all tomorrow, same time, same place!" The drama coach hopped off the stage, and the students shuffled into the hall.

Tim picked up Nikki's book bag and slung it over his shoulder. "I'll walk you to the parking lot," he said, holding open the door.

"You can do better than that," she said lightly, reaching into her purse for her keys. Remembering Lacey's advice, she tossed her key ring to him.

The shiny keys caught the sunlight and glinted as Tim snatched them from the air.

"I thought maybe you'd like to drive me home," Nikki told him.

Tim looked dumbfounded. "In your car?" he asked, staring at the key ring in his hand.

"Sure," Nikki replied.

Tim frowned. He fingered the key ring, then glanced toward the parking lot where Nikki's Camaro gleamed in the fading rays of the afternoon sun. "No, thanks," he said, tossing the keys back to Nikki.

She didn't react quickly enough, and the key ring dropped into the grass. "Why not?" she asked as she scooped up the keys.

Tim shrugged. "I just don't feel like it right now, that's all. Maybe some other time, okay?"

Nikki stared at him.

Avoiding her eyes, Tim added, "I should get home anyway."

Nikki's mouth dropped open. Hadn't Tim asked her out for a hamburger after rehearsal? "Oh, come on," she said, forcing a smile. "Live a little."

Tim's jaw tightened. "I can't," he said. "Look, Nikki, I've really got to run. I have a chemistry test tomorrow that I should start studying for."

"But . . ." Nikki said, then hesitated. "I thought we were on our way to get a burger."

"That was before I remembered the test," Tim replied, glancing away. "I really can't. Another time, though, okay?"

Nikki nodded. "Sure," she said flatly. "It's no big deal."

Tim smiled, but it looked forced.

Nikki wanted to dissolve into tears, but

her pride wouldn't let her. She wondered now if he still wanted to date her. She wondered if they were even going to the homecoming dance together.

"Nikki—" Tim began.

"Yes?" she said hopefully.

He paused, then handed Nikki her book bag. "I'll see you later," he told her. Turning quickly, he dashed across the lot to his mother's Ford Taurus, jumped inside, and started the engine. He drove out of the lot without even glancing back.

Nikki was stunned. What was going on? Tim had acted so cold and distant, just as he had the day before.

There had to be more to Tim's aversion to her car than simple pride or envy. There was something more, something Tim Cooper didn't want her to know about.

Nikki's hands were shaking as she unlocked the car door and slid inside. The plush interior felt hot against her skin, and the air was stuffy. Nikki plunged her key into the ignition and rolled down the window.

All the joy she'd experienced earlier had disappeared. The shiny lights on the digital dashboard seemed to taunt her. She stopped at the edge of the parking lot and caught a glimpse of her reflection in the rearview mirror. Her hair looked terrible, and her eyebrows were pulled into a worried line that creased her forehead.

"Stop it," Nikki told the self-pitying girl in the mirror. She wasn't going to let Tim Cooper go without a fight!

 **5**

Brittany kicked off her left shoe, and the red flat hit the back of her closet with a thud. She dreaded going to the stupid alumni meeting at Nancy Drew's house because Nikki Masters would be there as student coordinator.

Brittany yanked her sweater over her head and sighed. After flopping down on her bed, she stared up at the canopy. Her room was nice, she supposed, with its pretty striped wallpaper, frilly curtains, and canopied bed, but it was so ordinary.

"Hi, Brittany." Tamara, Brittany's younger sister, shoved the door open.

"What're you doing, spying on me again?" Brittany snapped, standing up.

"No," Tamara replied, breezing into the room and sitting on Brittany's desk chair. Tamara was a brainy thirteen-year-old with unruly brown hair and flashing dark eyes hidden behind thick glasses. She copied everything about Brittany, even to the point of borrowing Brittany's favorite jewelry and makeup.

Tamara leaned her elbows on her knees. "Where are you going?"

"To Nancy Drew's house." Brittany walked back to the closet to choose an outfit for the alumni gathering. She picked an oversize khaki skirt and blouse, a gold belt, and rust-colored suede boots. The belt made several loops around her small waist.

"Hey, I've never seen *that* before," Tamara said admiringly, pointing to Brittany's midsection.

Brittany glanced at her sister in the mirror. "Hands off. I just got it."

But Tamara's eyes were glued to the belt. Brittany knew her younger sister well enough to realize that within a few days the belt would suddenly be missing. She supposed she should be flattered that Tamara wanted to copy her, but sometimes she could be such a pain.

"Do you think you could get Nancy

Drew's autograph for me?" Tamara asked suddenly.

Brittany thought she might be sick. "Not a chance." She grabbed her notebook and purse and started for the door. "Remember, you're supposed to clean up the dinner dishes."

"I *hate* to do dishes!" Tamara complained.

"We all have to take turns, especially when Mom works late."

Tamara looked so glum that Brittany paused for a second to cheer her up. She really liked her sister—well, most of the time. "I'll tell you what," she said. "Tomorrow after school I'll show you how to French-braid your hair."

"I already know how." Tamara shrugged.

"I mean with more than one braid and some ribbons." Brittany fingered Tamara's unkempt brown strands. "Just in case you want to change your style."

"Okay," Tamara said, obviously pleased.

Brittany turned back for one last look in the mirror. After adjusting her skirt, Brittany was satisfied that she looked sensational. She intended to be the most gorgeous girl at Nancy Drew's house, and she was going to outshine Nikki Masters no matter what!

* * *

The Drew house, a gracious two-story home, was ablaze with lights. When Nikki knocked on the front door, she could hear voices and laughter filtering through a first-floor window.

"I was wondering when you'd show up," Nancy said as she opened the door. Her red-blond hair was pulled back into a ponytail, and her blue eyes glowed from the light in the hallway. "Don't tell me — you got lost on the way."

"Right," Nikki replied, laughing. She held up her camera case. "I hope you don't mind. I thought I'd take some pictures for the *Record.*"

"No problem," Nancy replied. "How about something to drink? We've got soda and iced tea."

"Anything," Nikki said.

Nancy led Nikki to the kitchen, handed her a can of cola, then walked her into the den. Several River Heights alumni whom Nikki recognized had already gathered and made themselves at home in the comfortable chairs and on the couch. The coffee table was laden with bowls of popcorn, peanuts, and chips, and quiet rock added musical background to the excited conversation.

"We've already started," Nancy said to

Nikki, nodding toward a red-haired young man with thick glasses. "That's Alan Sedgwick. He's my right-hand person on the committee. This is Peggy, and I guess you can read everyone else's name tag after you make your own." She handed Nikki an adhesive-backed tag and a felt pen and turned to the others. "Everyone, this is Nikki Masters, my next-door neighbor. She's our student coordinator."

"Lucky you," a deep voice drawled. Nikki's gaze traveled to the leather recliner, where a handsome young man was sitting with his feet dangling over the arm of the chair. The name on his tag was Jack Reilly, and he offered Nikki a lazy smile.

"I think I'm pretty lucky," Nikki replied. She was sure she'd seen Jack before, but where? Not at school. Tall and lean with wavy light brown hair and dark eyes, Jack seemed faintly amused at the hubbub in the Drew den. He was wearing faded jeans and a gray sweatshirt with a Westmoor University logo. It suddenly came to Nikki—she recognized him from the country club.

"Okay, everybody!" Alan stood in the center of the room just as the doorbell chimed.

Nancy headed for the front door as Alan

kept on talking. "Now, listen up, everybody. We have only a few days before homecoming, and we still have to plan our whole skit. Granted it'll only be ten or fifteen minutes long, but we want it to be great. Nancy and I have been talking, and we decided that this year we're going to do a spoof of football."

Nikki noticed that Jack Reilly was only half listening. His attention had strayed to the hallway. Nikki followed his gaze — straight to Brittany Tate. Nancy interrupted Alan to introduce her to the crowd.

Jack didn't actually whistle, but Nikki saw him suck in his breath a bit. Brittany, more gorgeous than usual, appeared radiant that night. Her long black hair swept her shoulders in gentle curls, her cheeks were pink, her brown eyes fairly danced behind a thick fringe of black lashes.

Every pair of eyes was directed her way, and she obviously enjoyed being in the spotlight.

"Hi, Brittany," one young woman called.

"You can sit over here," another said.

"No way," the guy behind her said. "She's sitting with me."

Did Brittany know everyone? Nikki wondered as Nancy offered Brittany a soda. To

Nikki's surprise, Brittany blushed and asked for Nancy's autograph—for her little sister. Maybe Brittany truly *had* changed. Nikki wanted to think so, because this stupid rivalry wasn't going to do anyone any good.

"Okay, back to business," Alan said, commanding their attention. "As I said, we've decided to spoof the football team, and we've come up with a great idea. Pete Fairbanks here"—he motioned to a lanky guy of about twenty-five—"is a carpenter. He says he can build our float, which will be a huge cake decorated like a football field."

"I'll do the carpentry," Pete said. "But I can't handle all that papier-mâché stuff."

"I'll do it," a young woman offered. "I'm an art student."

Alan nodded and scribbled on his clipboard. Nikki, too, was taking notes, as was Brittany.

"Cindy will make the papier-mâché figures," Alan said. "What about the banners?"

"I think I can handle those," a young woman named Jenny chimed in.

"Good. Remember, the slogan is 'River Heights Raiders—We take the cake,'" Alan reminded her.

"Got it," Jenny said.

Alan's gaze swept the room. "Now for the actual skit. We need a few volunteers."

Deep groans filled the den.

"Come on, come on," Alan said. "A few of us will act out a bungled football game. It won't be so tough."

"Count me out," Peter said emphatically.

Everyone laughed.

"No, no, it's going to be fun. A great time, really!" Alan insisted.

"I'd hate to see what he considers a bad time," Jack said loudly.

Alan looked annoyed. "For that one, Reilly, you're elected!"

The entire room applauded.

Jack's jaw dropped. "No way——"

"Put Jack's name down, Alan," Jenny said.

Jumping to his feet, Jack struck a pose. "If nominated, I will not run. If elected, I will not serve."

"Knock it off, Reilly! You'll be the head cheerleader," Alan said, scribbling on his clipboard again.

"Cheerleader?" Jack repeated over the laughter.

"Right," Alan said. "Now, we need a woman for the football captain. You'll both get to carry a couple of batons that will spew out confetti."

"I can see why a cheerleader might carry a baton. But why would a football captain carry one?" someone called out.

"No real reason. Just for effect—for the confetti."

"I'll do it—if Jack does," a pretty young woman seated near the window spoke up. Nikki had to read her name tag before recognizing Claire Halliday, a jazz singer who had graduated from River Heights High several years before.

Everyone clapped and Jack finally held up his hands in mock surrender. "Okay, okay, you win. I'll do it. But if this thing turns out to be a disaster, my name is Alan Sedgwick!"

Laughter rumbled through the room before Alan said, "Good, that's settled, then. Now, let's see. We have someone from the student body to help oversee the float, props, and costumes, right?"

Nancy's eye found Nikki's. "That's why we have a student coordinator, right, Nikki?"

"Right," Nikki responded. The room was filled with so much enthusiasm that she was happy to be a part of it.

"Great! Now we're getting somewhere."

Alan wrote furiously on his clipboard. "One more thing—because we're all so busy we need someone to help with the props."

"The home ec department said they'd help with the costumes," Claire reminded him.

"And don't forget Coach Jenkins," Jenny said. "He said we could use some old uniforms."

Nikki took a few notes as Nancy played hostess. She lugged in more soda pop and refilled the bowls of chips and popcorn.

Brittany, surveying the crowded room, smiled to herself. This meeting was going better than she'd hoped. Not only was the best-looking guy in the room watching her every move, but the alumni homecoming skit presented the perfect opportunity for her to put Nikki Masters in her place. She had to swallow a smug smile as she raised her hand and waved at Alan. "You know," she said, "my dad's kind of an inventor. I think he could come up with a gizmo to make the batons shoot confetti."

"An inventor? Really?" Alan pursed his lips thoughtfully.

Brittany nodded. "He works for Masters Electronics."

Alan's gaze slid to Nikki.

"That's right," Nikki said, shifting uncomfortably in her chair. "My father thinks Mr. Tate is the next Thomas Edison."

Brittany's smile widened. "I'm sure it won't be a problem for him."

Alan offered her a grateful smile, and Brittany felt a pang of remorse. Maybe she was pushing things too far.

Alan jotted down a note and nodded toward Brittany. "Thanks a lot. That would really help out. Well, I guess that's it. We'll take a break for a bit and then work on the skit."

Brittany jotted a few notes, grabbed another can of diet soda, and crossed the room to mingle with some of the alumni. Surprisingly, the meeting wasn't dull at all, especially since she had Jack Reilly as an audience to follow her every move. His attention definitely added some spice to the evening.

Brittany pretended not to notice Jack and flirted innocently with a couple of the other guys. Finally, however, she let him corner her near the window.

"So, how'd *you* get roped into this?" Jack asked, giving Brittany a crooked smile that caused her heart to thump crazily. "You did a lot of scribbling during the meeting."

Brittany suddenly felt tongue-tied as Jack's dark eyes searched her face. What was wrong with her? She flipped her hair over her shoulder. "I'm with the school paper," she told him. "I write 'Off the Record.'"

"What's that?" Jack raised his brows.

"Only the most popular column in the paper," Claire Halliday chimed in. "Don't you remember?"

Brittany smiled gratefully at Claire and told herself that she should start listening to jazz.

"I guess I always concentrated on the sports page," Jack admitted. His warm gaze swung back to Brittany's. "So tell me about your column."

Brittany widened her eyes. "Actually, I need to do a couple of interviews with alumni by tomorrow morning. That's my main reason for being here. How about you?"

Jack laughed. "I'm not all that interesting, believe me."

"I'm not so sure about that," Brittany said coyly. But before she became completely mesmerized by Jack, she turned to Claire. "And I'd love to talk to you, too."

Claire laughed. "As long as it's tonight. I'm flying out to L.A. tomorrow."

"But you'll be back for the game?" Brittany asked.

"Absolutely. I can't wait to see Jack make a fool of himself." Claire smiled.

"In your dreams, Halliday," Jack joked back as Claire moved toward the coffee table where Pete was planning the "cake." "Now, Ms. Tate, tell me all about you."

"I will," Brittany promised. "Right after my interviews."

Jack leaned back against the wall and crossed his arms over his chest. "Okay, shoot, but believe me, you'll be bored."

No way, Brittany thought. When Jack's fingers grazed her arm, she even temporarily forgot her plans to settle the score with Nikki.

Tonight, Brittany decided, she intended to concentrate on Jack Reilly!

6

Nikki dropped her books on the floor and fell onto her bed. Even though it was after ten o'clock, she picked up the phone and dialed Robin's number.

"Hello?" Robin answered breathlessly. "Cal?"

"No, Robin, it's me," Nikki told her.

"Oh." Robin sounded disappointed, but she quickly changed her tone. "What's up?"

Nikki told her all about the alumni meeting.

"Brittany Tate was there?" Robin said in surprise. "Why?"

"To interview some alumni and because she's one of the planners of the halftime show."

"You'd better watch that girl."

"Oh, she's okay," Nikki said, twisting the phone cord around her fingers.

"Yeah, if you don't mind walking around with a knife in your back," Robin said.

Nikki kicked off her shoes and shook out her hair. "Really, I think she's trying to change."

"I'll believe that when I see it," Robin replied. "So tell me, did Tim drive your car today?"

Nikki closed her eyes, remembering what had happened. "Hardly. Listen to this." She told Robin everything, including the way Tim got out of their date.

"Something's definitely bugging him," Robin decided. "Maybe—"

"How're things going with you and Calvin?" Nikki asked quickly.

"Okay, I guess," Robin said. "We see each other every night."

"That sounds wonderful," Nikki said.

"It is. Most of the time," Robin replied. "Cal picks me up every night after swim practice and we study chemistry and history together. My mom and dad like him, and you know *I'm* crazy about the guy." She sighed loudly.

"But . . . ?" Nikki prodded.

"Well, sometimes we fight," Robin admitted.

"Lacey's worried about you, you know," Nikki said. "And I'm worried, too," she added.

"Why?"

"You've been pretty wrapped up with Calvin. Maybe too wrapped up."

"I'm in love, Nikki. You should know what that means." Robin sounded annoyed.

"I do know," Nikki admitted, thinking of Tim and the on-again, off-again quality of their relationship the past few days.

"And as for Lacey, she spends a lot of time with Rick, doesn't she?" Robin continued.

Rick Stratton was Lacey's current boyfriend.

"Well, yes," Nikki admitted.

"Then . . . ?"

"Then maybe we shouldn't worry about you," Nikki said. Robin was beginning to sound like her old self again.

"I think you've got more than enough worries with Tim," Robin told her.

"I know," Nikki said, staring up at the ceiling as she lay on her bed.

"Look, Nik, I've really got to go," Robin said. "Calvin's probably been trying to call, and I'll die if I don't get to talk to him again tonight."

"Okay," Nikki said. "See you tomorrow. We're going shopping—don't forget." She hung up and stripped out of her clothes. Robin was fine, she told herself. And besides, she had problems of her own.

The next day at rehearsal Nikki watched as Kevin Hoffman, who was playing the Stage Manager in *Our Town,* doffed a pretend hat to a nonexistent audience. "Hmm . . . Eleven o'clock in Grover's Corners. You get a good rest, too. Good night."

"Bravo!" Mrs. Burns clapped loudly. "Great job! I'll see you all next week!"

Nikki let out a sigh. The rehearsal had gone very well. Unfortunately, she hadn't had a chance to talk to Tim yet, but she planned to find out right after rehearsal just what was bugging him. In homeroom and English, and now at rehearsal, he'd been friendly but distant. There hadn't been enough time or privacy to really pin him down and talk anyway.

"Hey, let's all go down to the Pizza Palace," Kevin suggested as the cast members began to slip on their jackets and grab their book bags. "I'm starved."

"You're always starved," Martin Salko told him. Martin played the part of Howie Newsome in the play.

Kevin took a swipe at Martin's shoulder.

"Okay, I could go for some pizza right now," Lara Bennett said. Lara, a sophomore, played the part of Mrs. Gibbs. With her straight cinnamon-brown hair and freckles, she hardly looked right for the role of a middle-aged woman. But she could act the part very well. "Nikki, how about you?"

Nikki shrugged, scanning the small crowd for Tim. "Sure, why not? I can drive."

"Great!" Lara tucked her script into her large Kenya straw bag. "I need a ride."

"Hey, where's Cooper?" Martin asked.

"He took off already," Lara replied. "He said something about homework, I think."

Nikki's heart plummeted. Was Tim actually *avoiding* her? Suddenly she had no interest in pizza or in anything else. She couldn't let another minute pass without sorting matters out with Tim—one way or the other. She tucked her purse under her arm. Maybe, if she hurried, she could catch up with him.

"You're still going for pizza, aren't you?" Lara asked anxiously.

"Sure I am," Nikki replied, "but I really

need to speak to Tim for a minute. I'll meet you at my car, okay? It's the blue—"

"I know which one it is," Lara said. "The whole school does."

Nikki winced on her way out the door. "Right." Wondering what she would say to Tim if she managed to catch up with him, she jogged toward the parking lot. It was now or never, she told herself. This whole car thing was just plain stupid!

But as she reached the edge of the lot, Nikki saw Tim's mother's car disappearing around the corner. "He's driving so slowly, I could probably catch him on foot!" she muttered angrily, kicking at a pebble on the ground. One day Tim told her he loved her, and the next he gave her the cold shoulder. Well, she was sick of it!

"Hey, Nikki, wait up!" Robin, her hair still damp from the shower, dashed down the steps of the gym. "I thought you'd gone hours ago!"

"Play practice," Nikki said.

Robin ran her fingers through her wet locks. "What's going on?" she asked, her smooth forehead creasing as she took in Nikki's expression. "Uh-oh. You look like you could spit nails."

"I wish!"

"The trouble with Tim, huh?" Robin asked sympathetically.

Nikki knew her cheeks were flaming. "It's everything I told you last night and more." She sniffed and blinked back tears. "I'm just so unsure of Tim. Sometimes I think he's in love with me, and other times . . ." She rolled her eyes.

Robin's dark gaze grew serious. "I understand, believe me."

"I just don't get it," Nikki went on. "Most of the time Tim is perfect, but sometimes during the past couple of days he's acted as if I didn't even exist. It's like riding a roller coaster—one minute up, the next down."

"Maybe he's not the guy for you," Robin offered, shifting her books.

"Maybe not," Nikki agreed glumly. But if Tim *wasn't* right for her, why did her pulse leap at the sight of him? Why did she spend every night lying awake thinking about him? Why did her skin tingle whenever he touched her?

Robin bit her lip. "Love is unpredictable, Nikki."

Nikki felt as if she were missing something. The faraway look in Robin's eyes worried her. Robin always had her feet planted firmly on the ground. Or at least she used to—until she fell so hard for Calvin Roth.

"Hey, there you are!" Lara cried, running up to Nikki and Robin. "Did you catch up with Tim?"

"No," Nikki said with a sigh.

Lara frowned. "Listen, Nikki, if you don't want to go——"

"Of course I want to go," Nikki broke in, managing a weak smile. No guy, not even Tim Cooper, was going to make her life miserable! She unlocked the door of her Camaro. "Want to come along, Robin? The cast's having pizza down at the Palace."

"I'd like to," Robin said hesitantly, "but I'd better wait for Calvin."

"The invitation's for him, too," Nikki teased. "He can join us if he wants."

"Thanks, but not right now," Robin replied, her gaze sliding toward the gym. "But we still have a date to go shopping later, right?"

Nikki nodded. "Absolutely." Maybe she'd forget about her troubles with Tim by escaping to the mall.

"I'll call you later, okay?" Robin said.

"Oh, Robin, come on," Nikki pressed. "Why don't you come with us now? Then you and I can drive to the mall after three or four slices of double cheese and Canadian bacon. Calvin will understand."

"Nah." Robin shook her head, her dark hair sweeping her cheek. "I promised Calvin I'd wait for him."

That was a first. Robin never hung around waiting for a guy.

"Hey, there he is now! See ya." Robin took off and met Calvin at his car. They kissed as if they hadn't seen each other in weeks.

"Wow," said Lara.

Nikki didn't answer. Climbing behind the wheel, she unlocked Lara's door, then inserted the key into the ignition. The engine started smoothly.

"Awesome," Lara murmured. "I can't wait until I get my license." She ran her fingers along the dash, then leaned back against the plush seat. "You're so lucky," she told Nikki as they drove away from the school. "I bet every kid in River Heights would cut off his right arm for a car like this."

All but one, Nikki thought morosely. Tim Cooper wouldn't be caught dead in this Camaro!

* * *

"Okay, so tell us! Who's going to be in the alumni skit?" Kevin bit into a slice of pepperoni and olive pizza.

Nikki grinned. "Just the usual River Heights celebrities."

"Nancy Drew," Martin guessed.

Nikki nodded.

"And Bobby Shoenborn?"

"Nope. He's already started training camp with that pro basketball team," Nikki replied.

She was beginning to enjoy herself, even though Tim wasn't there. The Pizza Palace, decorated with red lacquered tables and a gleaming black-and-white tile floor, was buzzing. Waiters and waitresses whisked between the tables with huge trays of pizza and frothy mugs of root beer. Music blasted Bent Fender's latest hit from hidden speakers.

Lara picked up a piece of stringy double cheese pizza. "What about Claire Halliday? Will she be in it?"

"She'll be there," Nikki answered, picking the pepperoni off her slice and popping it into her mouth.

Lara's eyes sparkled. "She is *sooo* great. I heard she's getting a big new contract with some record company."

"Give me a break," Kevin said, wrinkling his nose. "I heard her sing 'The Star Spangled Banner' at one of our home games, and I barely recognized it."

Nikki giggled.

But Lara said defensively, "That's because you don't understand real art, Kevin. For your information, Claire Halliday could become one of the greatest jazz singers in this country!"

Kevin snorted. "I'll take country and western over jazz any day."

"You would?" Nikki asked, smothering a smile.

Kevin nodded. "You bet."

Nikki plucked a black Stetson from a nearby hat rack and plopped it neatly onto Kevin's head. It dropped nearly to his eyebrows.

"Hey! What—" Kevin started to protest. Then, realizing he was the center of attention, he began to clown around, mouthing the words to a Top 40 hit playing on the jukebox.

Nikki nearly choked on her root beer. "You missed your calling," she told him when she could breathe again.

Kevin twirled the hat on his hand, then dropped it back on the rack. "Enough of

this," he said. "I've got to get home. The
books call."

Martin swallowed the last of his soft
drink. "I'm out of here, too."

Nikki checked her watch. They'd been at
the Pizza Palace for an hour and a half.
"We'd better get moving," she said to Lara.
Briefly, she wondered if Tim had called
while she was gone—though deep in her
heart, she knew he hadn't. He knew where
she was, and he obviously hadn't wanted to
be with her.

As the two girls stepped outside, a chill
breeze whipped Nikki's hair into her face.
The sky was dark, and fat raindrops were
falling steadily from the swollen clouds.
Great, she thought. This was all she needed
to feel perfectly gloomy.

Mr. Tate studied his daughter thoughtfully. "You want me to do what?" he asked.

What was wrong with him? Brittany wondered. Had he gone deaf? She brushed the
dust off an old picnic bench in the garage and
sat down on it. The garage doors were closed,
and the sound of rain peppering the roof was
magnified in the small space. "Come on,
Dad," she wheedled. "It can't be that tough.
I just need four batons."

"And you want them to shoot shaving cream?" Mr. Tate looked skeptical.

"Right. They're props for a homecoming skit we're working on," Brittany explained patiently. "You know, for the halftime show."

Her father nodded, rubbing his chin. "I suppose I could rig something up."

"Sure you can! You're the best inventor in River Heights!" Brittany said brightly, bouncing up.

"By Saturday night?" Mr. Tate asked. He frowned, sitting down. "And it has to be shaving cream?" He picked up a pencil and began to sketch something quickly.

That was a good sign. Brittany knew she'd intrigued him. "Or something like shaving cream," she suggested. "If shaving cream won't work, how about some of that gooey string stuff?"

Mr. Tate's bushy dark brows shot up. "Gooey string?"

"You know what I mean," Brittany told him. "Tamara had some of it last Christmas. It's plastic and comes in a tube. Kind of like toothpaste."

Mr. Tate chuckled. "I remember," he said. "Tamara got it all over one of your mother's poinsettias and she ended up in big trouble."

Brittany didn't want to be reminded about that. Their mother had been livid, and poor Tamara had been grounded for a week. "Maybe we'd better not use gooey string," Brittany said.

Mr. Tate nodded. "Shaving cream might be safer."

"Definitely." Brittany dropped a kiss on her father's head and went out the garage door. She could see the thick white shaving foam now, shooting out all over a shocked Claire Halliday and Jack Reilly.

But as she darted through the rain to the kitchen, Brittany felt a tiny twinge of remorse. Jack was really cute and he did act as if he liked her. She hated to play a dirty trick on him. But then, he'd never know it was she, would he? If everything went according to her plan, Miss High-and-Mighty Nikki Masters would take the rap for this one! And as for Claire Halliday, who cared? Besides, the publicity might even be good for her career.

Tamara was seated at the kitchen table, her math book open with a candy bar beside it. She glanced up when Brittany entered the room. "You promised!" she said.

"Promised?" Brittany asked. What was the little twerp talking about now?

"French braids, remember?"

Brittany clapped a hand to her head. "Oh, I forgot. I'm sorry. How about right now?"

"How about right after she finishes her homework?" Mrs. Tate spoke up. A short, pretty woman whose dark hair was streaked with gray, she was arranging flowers near the sink. She owned and managed a flower shop in the mall. The Tate house always smelled of carnations, roses, or mums.

"I *hate* algebra!" Tamara groaned.

Mrs. Tate laughed. "I'll let you in on a little secret, honey. So did I."

Grumbling loudly, Tamara turned back to her homework.

"Just let me know when you're ready," Brittany said sweetly.

"It'll be never," Tamara said.

Brittany shrugged. "Well, come and get me when you're done, squirt."

With that, Brittany walked down the short hallway to her bedroom, humming to herself. She could hardly wait for homecoming.

 **7**

"My feet are killing me!" Nikki complained, dropping onto a bench near the fountain in the middle of Southside Mall.

The mall was a madhouse. Lured by a series of sales that would last until midnight, huge crowds of people were nudging and shoving their way along the quarry-tiled floor and into the various shops and boutiques.

Nikki wedged off one navy pump with the toe of her other shoe. "Why didn't I wear my running shoes?" she muttered.

"Because you're looking for something dressy," Robin reminded her. "And believe me, running shoes are not a fashion statement."

"Okay, okay." Nikki smiled without much enthusiasm. So far, she didn't even have a date for homecoming. Everyone assumed she was going with Tim and didn't bother to ask her. At least that was what she told herself to feel better about her dateless state.

"Come on." Robin tugged on Nikki's hand and dragged her to her feet. "Let's try Glad Rags. They always have just the right thing."

"That store is about five miles west," Nikki grumbled.

"It's only half a block, right down this corridor." Robin started winding her way through the crowd.

Sighing, Nikki shoved her foot back into the tight pump and ran to catch up with her friend.

"You know what your problem is?" Robin asked, giving her a knowing look over her shoulder.

"I have a problem?" Nikki arched her eyebrows.

"Yep. At least one. Maybe more," Robin assured her.

Nikki rolled her eyes. "I don't think I want to hear this."

"Well, I think you need to let off some steam. You know, put all of your energy into something besides the play and Tim Cooper. You should get into sports, Nikki.''

"I play tennis," Nikki said defensively, trying to keep up with her long-legged friend.

"Well, the swim team could use an anchor for the relays.''

"And that's just what I'd be," Nikki told her. "An anchor. I'd sink right to the bottom of the pool.''

Robin laughed and stopped suddenly. Nikki plowed into her. "Listen, Nik, all I'm saying is, maybe you shouldn't get so wrapped up in one guy," Robin said, leading Nikki over to Glad Rags.

"Look who's talking," Nikki teased.

Robin shrugged. "Calvin's different. Hey, here we are!" she said, glancing at the window of Glad Rags. "Look at that dress!" Robin's eyes grew round as she stared at a mannequin wearing an emerald green dress. It had huge sleeves that narrowed to a cuffless hem at the elbow and an oversize bodice that nipped into a small waist. "It's positively me!"

Nikki followed Robin into the store. The dress *was* terrific.

Within minutes, Robin had talked to the saleswoman, found the dress in her size, and ducked into a fitting room.

Twirling in front of the mirror, she grinned at her reflection. The green dress, accentuated with a wide black belt, fit her perfectly. And the black enamel earrings and bracelet she had picked out added the perfect touch. She'd have to buy new black patent shoes—flats because Calvin was an inch or two shorter than Robin.

"It's gorgeous," Nikki said breathily.

A pink flush lit up Robin's cheeks. "Do you think Calvin will like it?"

"I don't see how he could help but," Nikki replied.

Fingering the skirt, Robin said softly, "You know, Nik, I can't believe what's happened to me. I never thought I'd fall in love so soon." She sighed. "But all I want to do these days is be with Calvin."

"It's that serious?" Nikki asked, feeling a bit envious.

Robin nodded. "Oh, Nikki, Calvin is just *so* great. I know this sounds crazy, but I think he might be *the one*—forever!"

Nikki couldn't believe what she was hearing. Calvin and Robin hadn't been going together long enough for Robin to decide this. "Really?" she said carefully.

"Really. And it's pretty scary. But he's all

I ever think about—except swimming, of course."

"Of course," Nikki said doubtfully. Now she was beginning to worry about Robin. Maybe Lacey had been right. Romantic obsession wasn't her style. It might not be healthy. "What about school?"

"I'm not a complete idiot," Robin replied. "I know school's important!" Robin looked down at her feet, then glanced back up and caught Nikki's reflection in the mirror. "I've never felt this way before, Nik." Then, as if she had suddenly become aware of what she was saying, she grinned. As soon as she had changed, she grabbed Nikki by the shoulders and marched her out of the dressing room. "Enough of all this talk about me! You have work to do."

"Me?"

"Yeah, you are ordered to go out and find one sensational drop-dead outfit," she commanded in a stern voice.

"Aye, aye, Captain!" Nikki gave a mock salute, then rummaged through the racks until she found an outfit that consisted of a short black skirt that buttoned up the front, a hot pink off-the-shoulder top, and a black and pink leather-trimmed jacket.

"Well?" she asked Robin, once she'd tried on the three pieces.

Robin shook her head. "The navy shoes don't work."

"I know that!" Nikki said, a little annoyed.

"You need something to tie the whole outfit together," Robin said. "Wait a minute. I saw just the thing—" With Nikki trailing her, Robin headed for the display case near the cash register. "There!" Robin triumphantly pointed a finger at a black-and-silver belt. "Sensational! You'll drive Tim crazy!"

I doubt it, Nikki thought unhappily. Tim probably wouldn't even see the outfit.

They paid for their purchases, then ambled through the mall looking at the window displays until they reached Platters, the record store where Lacey worked.

They went inside and immediately spotted Lacey talking to a short girl with black hair that hung past her waist. "I've heard three of the cuts from the new album," Lacey was saying, "and they're great. The way I figure it, you can never go wrong with Casey Michaels. Even if you don't like the music, there's a to-die-for poster inside."

The girl brightened, her smile widening to

show off a network of wires straightening her teeth. "Okay, I'll take the compact disk."

"You've got it!" Lacey rang up the sale and thanked the girl, then looked up to see Robin and Nikki. "Perfect timing," she said. "I go on my break in five minutes."

"We'll meet you down at Mocha and More," Nikki suggested.

"Good. Order me a cherry soda, a maple bar, and a raspberry fritter!"

"Ugh. Don't tell me, another health food kick," Robin said, shaking her head as she and Nikki headed out of the store.

Fifteen minutes later the girls were huddled around a small table in the café. Plants hung from the high ceiling, and the scent of java wafted through the single room. Though Mocha and More specialized in exotic coffees and rich chocolate desserts, a selection of fabulous pastries was always available.

"So what're you guys doing here?" Lacey asked, munching on her fritter.

"Robin needed a new dress for the dance," Nikki explained. She swirled the straw in her diet cola, then took a bite from Robin's pastry.

"So did Nikki," Robin added.

Lacey eyed Robin's and Nikki's plastic

shopping bags. "Glad Rags—my favorite!" She grinned at Nikki. "So Tim finally came through and asked you to the dance."

"No." Nikki scowled into her drink.

Lacey's happy expression dissolved into disappointment. "Are you two fighting?"

"I don't think so," Nikki replied. "I wish I knew what was happening."

"Oh, Nikki," Lacey said. "That's terrible. Maybe he's taking it for granted that you're going with him."

Nikki pushed her bangs from her eyes. "Well, I wish he'd tell me if that's the way he thinks. Robin and I got some great outfits, anyway."

Robin agreed. "Hey, Lace, remember that terrific green dress in the window?" She reached into her bag and withdrew her purchase. "Ta-da!"

Lacey's mouth fell open. "It's gorgeous!" She examined the dress and accessories, and Nikki's purchases as well. "This is absolutely depressing," she murmured enviously.

"Why?"

"Because I'm trying to save my money for a car, and I'd like a new outfit, too," Lacey said, sighing.

"Live a little," Robin told her. "You deserve a splurge."

Lacey shook her head. "No way. I've

wanted a car *forever,* and I'm going to get one." She slid one last glance at Nikki's skirt and top. "Even if it kills me."

"But you are going to the dance, aren't you?" Robin asked.

"With Rick." Lacey had no control over the smile that slowly spread across her face. "I can't wait! Maybe we can go out together after the dance."

"Sure," Robin replied.

Nikki watched the ice cubes dance in her diet soda. "I'm not sure I'll go," she said.

"What?" Lacey demanded. "But you're student coordinator for the alumni skit. You *have* to go. Not everyone goes with a date."

"Everyone who's a junior or senior always goes with a date," Nikki said, reminding them.

"I still think you can go," Lacey interjected. She pushed aside the rest of her dessert and, resting her elbows on the table, propped her chin in her hands. "You can come with us. Okay, out with it—what's the problem with Tim?"

"I don't know," Nikki said sadly.

Lacey blew a strand of red hair out of her eyes. "Is he still bugged about your car?"

"I don't know," Nikki answered again. She told her friends about Tim's strange behavior over the past couple of days.

"What's wrong with that guy?" Lacey asked, shaking her head.

Nikki shrugged. "I don't know," she said for the last time.

"If I were you, I'd just call Tim and ask what the problem is," Robin said simply. "The way I see it, you've got to. You can't be in limbo all the time."

"That's a little drastic," Lacey said, frowning.

"No, it's not," Robin insisted. "If Nikki wants a relationship with Tim, I mean a real one, she's got to get a few things straight with him! Otherwise it's all over."

"Over?" Nikki cried.

Lacey skewered Robin with a look that said, *Keep your big mouth shut!* "Since when are you the authority on love?"

Robin shrugged. "Well, I *do* have a serious boyfriend now."

"Oh, brother." Lacey polished off the last of her drink. "If you ask *me*," she advised Nikki, "I'd suggest being a little more subtle. But Robin is right. You do have to talk to Tim—"

"Thanks a lot," Robin muttered.

Lacey ignored her. "But be careful, Nikki. It does sound as if he's hiding something from you."

Nikki's stomach twisted. She wanted to

disagree with Lacey, but she couldn't. Hadn't she suspected the very same thing?

"Tim has been awfully secretive ever since he came to River Heights," Lacey went on.

"He's shy," Nikki protested.

"Nope." Robin shook her head. "Shy people don't try out for the romantic lead in the school play."

"Good point," Lacey said, nodding.

Robin finished her soda. "Anyway, you've got to find out what Tim's keeping from you, Nikki. And soon."

"I guess so," Nikki agreed reluctantly. "But I'm kind of afraid."

"Of what?" Robin asked.

Lacey pursed her lips. "Try to be a little sensitive, will you? Obviously, Nikki's worried that Tim will break up with her or something awful like that."

"Oh." Robin looked apologetic.

"It's all right," Nikki said quickly. "You're both right. I just have to get up the nerve to call Tim."

"Do it right away," Robin advised. "That way it won't be hanging over your head forever."

Nikki sighed. "Okay," she said aloud. "I'll do it." She shoved her half-eaten éclair aside. "I'll have things out with Tim Cooper tomorrow!"

8 〜〜〜

Nikki wiped her sweaty palms on her jeans, shook out her hands, then picked up the receiver and dialed Tim's number. Leaning back on the pillows of her bed, she silently counted the rings on the other end of the line. Nikki had wanted to speak to Tim in school that Thursday, but no opportunity presented itself. Now it was almost ten o'clock on Thursday night, and Nikki knew it was now or never.

"Hello?"

Nikki's thumping heart kicked into overdrive at the sound of Tim's voice. "Hi, Tim," she said. Her voice was much higher than she'd ever heard it. She cleared her throat.

"Nikki!"

Was it her imagination or did he really

sound glad to hear from her? "I, uh, didn't get a chance to talk to you yesterday or today after practice," she said. Nervously, she twisted the telephone cord around her fingers.

"I'm sorry," Tim was saying. "I've had a lot of homework."

"That's all right. Well, actually, it isn't," Nikki said, then groaned inwardly. Now she was off on the wrong foot! "I mean, I really wanted to talk to you."

"What's up?" Tim asked.

Nikki took a deep breath. "Tim, I don't understand what's going on," she said. "One minute I think you like me, and the next—"

"You know I like you, Nikki," Tim said. "I more than like you."

"Then why have you been avoiding me like the plague?" she asked.

Tim cleared his throat. "I haven't been—"

"Yes, you have," Nikki insisted. "Ever since I got my new car, you've been acting different!"

Tim didn't say a word. The seconds ticked by like years. Nikki felt hot tears of anger and frustration burning behind her eyes.

Still Tim said nothing.

Finally Nikki couldn't stand the tense

silence any longer. She forced the words from her throat. "I care about you a lot, Tim. I really do. But I have to know what you're thinking, what's wrong between us."

"Nothing's wrong," he snapped.

Nikki closed her eyes and swallowed hard, trying to keep her voice even. "I feel as if you've been keeping something from me."

Tim paused. "Like what?"

Nikki's heart skipped a beat. This was going horribly! "That's why I need to talk to you," Nikki said, feeling a little desperate.

"Oh, Nikki," Tim said. "I've just had a lot on my mind lately. Lots of homework, the play, you. But nothing's wrong. *Really.*"

A huge lump formed in Nikki's throat.

"I've been too wrapped up in myself, I guess," Tim admitted, "and I'm sorry if I hurt you. I didn't mean to."

Nikki made a helpless little sound and instantly hated herself for it.

"How about if we go to Commotion tomorrow night?" Tim suggested suddenly. "I promise I'll be attentive and charming and—"

"Just be yourself," Nikki cut in, dashing aside the tears that had begun to slip from her eyes.

"Then it's a date?"

"Sure," she choked out. Tim still cared!

"I'll see you in school tomorrow. Oh, is seven all right tomorrow night?"

"Great."

"Nikki?" Mrs. Masters knocked gently on the door and poked her head into the room. "I came up to say good night. Honey, are you okay?"

Nikki tried to hide her tears. Nodding quickly to her mother, she told Tim, "Listen, I've really got to go."

"No problem," he replied. "See you at school tomorrow."

"Okay. 'Bye."

"You've been crying," her mother said gently after Nikki hung up.

"It's nothing. I-I'm just happy."

Mrs. Masters raised her eyebrows.

"Okay, okay," Nikki conceded. "Tim and I had a little misunderstanding, but it's over. We're going out tomorrow night."

"And everything's all right now?"

Nikki nodded emphatically. "Things couldn't be better," she said, pushing aside any lingering doubts.

"If they're so great, then why were you crying?" her mother asked.

"It's complicated," Nikki told her. "But

everything's going to be okay." She was beginning to believe the words herself. Hadn't Tim sounded as if he missed her?

"If you say so." Mrs. Masters walked back to the door. "I'll say good night now." She paused. "Nikki, if there's ever anything bothering you and you want to talk, just let me know."

"I will," Nikki promised as her mother closed the door behind her.

"You'll see," Nikki whispered to herself. "Everything's going to work out!"

At lunch on Friday Brittany stared down at her taco salad. The cafeteria chili had already made the lettuce soggy, and the cheese had melted into a gooey mess. What a disaster!

"Looks like the cook is keeping us on our diets again," Kim Bishop announced, picking at the dark wilted lettuce.

Samantha Daley set her tray down at their table. Then, tossing her hair back, she scanned the boys in the lunchroom. "Got a date for the dance yet, Brittany?" she asked.

Brittany arched one eyebrow. "Not yet. But you know how choosy I am. I may decide by tonight."

"So who's the lucky guy going to be?"

Brittany shrugged. "You'll just have to wait to find out like everyone else." Actually, she had no idea who her date would be.

"This sounds interesting," Samantha said. "Come on, Brittany, who is it? Tim Cooper?"

Brittany waved away that suggestion with a flip of her hand. "Not interested."

Kim laughed. "You mean, you're not interested in *him,* or he's not interested in *you?*"

Brittany forced a frozen smile. "I could have him *if* I wanted him, but I'm moving on to new territory now."

"Like who?" Kim asked.

Brittany smiled slyly. "Someone more mature." To avoid her friends' eyes, she looked around the crowded cafeteria. In one corner, as far from everyone else as possible, a group of kids in leather jackets and spiked hair were huddled. The jocks sat in the center, laughing and joking loudly, and the brains sat near the far wall. Always the same.

Brittany's gaze moved to the huge bank of windows. There Nikki Masters and her friends were giggling over something. Sunlight streamed through the glass, highlighting Nikki's sun-streaked hair. Brittany smiled in spite of herself. She couldn't wait for homecoming!

Then Brittany looked up and saw Tim Cooper, as devastatingly gorgeous as ever, sauntering past her table. Tim didn't even look at Brittany. He was in a hurry to get to Nikki. She waved to him, and he puppy-dogged over.

Brittany squeezed her eyes closed for a second. Tim's fascination with Nikki was sickening.

When she opened her eyes, she found Kim staring at her. "What's gotten into you?" Kim asked.

"This lunch," Brittany lied. "I don't know how they get away with calling it food. You'd think the Board of Health would intervene."

Samantha smothered a smile. "Lunch here is always lousy."

"I suppose." Brittany sighed. All around her, kids were laughing and talking and there was a kind of electricity in the air for homecoming the next day. A huge blue-and-white poster proclaimed boldly: "Tame the Bears." Another sign announced the half-time festivities.

"I was in the gym earlier," Samantha said, picking apart her ham sandwich and removing all traces of lettuce. "It looked great."

Brittany's mood lifted slightly. "Mmm. We should have a terrific parade, too!"

"How's halftime coming along?" Samantha asked.

Brittany felt one corner of her lips curve up. "It should be interesting."

"Fat chance!" Jeremy Pratt dropped into an empty chair near Kim. He tossed his utensils off his tray and scowled. "If you ask me, homecoming's going to be one big yawn, as it is every year."

"Not this year," Brittany said as she thought of shaving cream splattering everyone in the skit. "Trust me, it'll be anything but dull."

"I'll believe it when I see it," Kim said.

Brittany leaned forward. "Don't miss the halftime skit," she advised.

DeeDee Smith set her tray down next to Samantha's. "Hey, good job," she said to Brittany, slapping a copy of the *Record* onto the table. "Those interviews were just what we needed. I didn't have to edit any of it."

"They were your idea," Brittany reminded her, but she felt warmed by the praise. At least DeeDee appreciated her.

"I know," DeeDee replied with a laugh. "Maybe that's why I liked them so much."

"What are you talking about?" Samantha

scooped up the paper and flipped to the social page. Brittany's column, "Off the Record," was longer than usual.

The interviews with Nancy Drew, Claire Halliday, and Jack Reilly surrounded the main article and were supplemented by old yearbook pictures.

"Hey! This guy is cute!" Samantha said, pointing to a two-year-old shot of Jack.

Brittany frowned as she studied the picture. It didn't really do Jack justice. He looked like such a *boy*. Now his jaw had become more defined and his features more angular. "You should see him now," she said.

"I'd love to," Samantha drawled.

"He'll be at homecoming," Brittany replied. She wanted to tell Samantha "hands off," but she didn't have any real claim on Jack Reilly—not yet, anyway. Maybe she could get *him* for her date to the dance. . . .

"Uh-oh, don't look now," Kim whispered, "but Mr. Head-of-Homecoming is heading this way."

Brittany groaned inwardly. Ben Newhouse, president of the junior class, was nice enough, but he was a stickler for detail. A clipboard was tucked under his arm as usual, and Brittany was reminded of a drill sergeant ready to call the roll.

"Hi, Britt," he said.

Brittany cringed at the way he butchered her name but tried to look interested.

"I checked the floats, the band, and the costumes," Ben said. "Everything's right on schedule."

"I know," Brittany told him.

"What about the cheerleaders?" he asked.

"What about them?" Christina Martinez, cocaptain of the cheerleading squad, called from the table behind Brittany.

"Are you guys ready?" Ben asked.

Chris nodded. "Yep. We've got a great new cheer, complete with pyramid and back flips."

Ben made a huge check on his clipboard.

"The pyramid was Brittany's idea," Chris added with her pretty all-American smile.

"Good job!" Ben offered Brittany a smile.

"Thanks," she replied, looking down modestly.

Jeremy Pratt's eyes were on Brittany as she picked up her tray. "Maybe you're right," he said. "Maybe homecoming will finally be interesting this year."

"I personally guarantee it." Brittany carried her tray back to the kitchen. As she started toward her locker, she spied Nikki Masters heading her way. What now? she wondered, panicking a little. Had Nikki found out about her plan? But she couldn't have. *No one* knew. "Hi, Nikki," Brittany said, forcing a cheery grin.

"Hi," Nikki replied. "I've been looking for you."

"Oh?" Brittany gulped. "What's up?"

"I read your column and interviews in the paper. They were really great."

"Thanks," Brittany said, relieved. She meant it. Maybe Nikki wasn't so bad after all. At least she recognized exceptional writing talent.

"I've got everything together for the alumni skit," Nikki went on, "except the batons. Are they ready?"

"They will be," Brittany said brightly. "My dad's just about finished, but he's had to work late a few nights. I probably won't be able to get them to you until just before the skit."

"No problem," Nikki replied. "As long as they work."

"Oh, they'll work," Brittany assured her.

"Good. And thanks, Brittany. You've been

a big help." Nikki waved and hurried down the hall.

Brittany didn't move until Nikki had blended into the crowd. Then she sagged against the wall. Maybe she was making a big mistake—maybe she shouldn't make an enemy of Nikki Masters.

She bit her lip, paralyzed with indecision. "Why were you talking to *her?*" Kim Bishop asked, coming up and startling Brittany from her thoughts.

"Oh, she was asking me about homecoming stuff. She liked my interviews."

"She did?" Kim said in surprise. "Well, what did you expect her to say? Personally, I don't know why you put yourself out for that two-bit rag. No one even appreciates you."

Brittany frowned. Hadn't both DeeDee and Nikki congratulated her on a job well done?

"And as for Nikki," Kim continued, "she's just a big phony."

"Well, I know, but—" Brittany began.

"Hey, what's with you?" Kim asked. Her eyes narrowed. "Are you buying into Nikki's act? All that cozying up to the little people? Well, it makes me sick."

For a strange moment, Brittany almost felt like defending Nikki.

"Face it, Brittany, Nikki has it all," Kim swept on. "The best-looking boyfriend in school, a hot new car, and more money than the rest of us will see in a lifetime."

The bell rang and Brittany jumped. Humiliation and injustice cut right to her heart all over again. Nikki had shown Brittany up time and time again. But not on homecoming night, Brittany remembered. Then it would be Nikki Masters's turn to look like a fool!

9

Nikki's heart was soaring. Looking through the living room window, she could see Tim pulling into the drive in his mother's car. Then her heart fell. He wasn't alone. A boy she didn't recognize was sitting in the passenger seat.

"Tim's here," she called over her shoulder, hoping her mother would hear. "I'll be home before midnight."

"See you later, dear," Mrs. Masters replied from somewhere near the kitchen. "Have a nice time."

Nikki grabbed her purse and slipped her arms through the sleeves of her jean jacket just as the front bell chimed.

Opening the door, she found Tim shifting

nervously from one foot to the other. He was wearing white cords and a royal blue shirt. His gaze found hers and lingered on her face. "You look great," he said, taking her hand.

"So do you," Nikki said simply.

Tim laughed. "Thanks. Come on, let's go." He started down the flagstone path, then glanced at the car parked in the circular drive. His footsteps slowed. "Listen, Nikki, I forgot to tell you that Carl's coming with us tonight."

"Carl?" Nikki raised her eyebrows.

"Carl Schmidt, a friend of mine from Chicago. I knew he was coming to visit sometime soon, but I wasn't exactly sure when. He just showed up a couple of hours ago, and I guess he'll be here for the weekend."

"Oh." Nikki hoped her disappointment wasn't too obvious.

"That's okay, isn't it?" he asked, sounding genuinely concerned.

"Sure," Nikki replied, managing a smile. Now any hopes she'd had for a romantic weekend with Tim were completely dashed.

Tim must have sensed how she was feeling. "Nikki, he's my best friend," he explained. "And I didn't know how to bring this whole thing up to you. That's why I've been so moody lately."

Nikki could hardly believe her ears. Tim wasn't mad at her!

"I couldn't make any definite dates with you until Carl actually got here," Tim added.

"And that's why you've been avoiding me?" Nikki asked, puzzled.

"I haven't been avoiding you," Tim insisted. "I just didn't want Carl to feel left out or anything."

Nikki felt instant relief. She didn't really want to share Tim with Carl, but she was glad he had such a good friend. "Don't worry about it," Nikki told him. "The three of us will have a great time at Commotion."

Tim's lips twisted into a half-smile. "Sure."

They reached the car, and Tim opened the door for Nikki. After quick introductions, Carl climbed into the back seat and Nikki sat as close to Tim as her seat belt allowed.

As usual, Tim drove very slowly. Cars passed them, and one driver even honked, but Tim didn't seem to notice.

Nikki wanted to say something, but she held her tongue. She shot a quick glance back at Carl, but Tim's driving didn't seem to bother him in the least.

Carl had coffee brown hair and brown eyes, and he chatted with Tim incessantly. Leaning forward, his hands on the front seat, he talked steadily about kids Nikki had never even heard Tim mention. Tim laughed and nodded, and Nikki felt completely out of it.

She realized then just how little she really knew about Tim. Who, besides Carl and Yvette, had been his close friends? What was his old school like? Besides drama, what activities had he been interested in? Did he play any sports?

Nikki glanced his way. Tim's face, lit only by the dashboard lights, was more animated than she'd ever seen it. Though his eyes never left the road, Tim participated in Carl's outrageous stories by laughing and adding an occasional comment.

Nikki had a feeling it was going to be an interesting evening.

Commotion was jammed. The main dance floor was wall-to-wall kids moving to the throbbing beat of a local heavy-metal band that was the warm-up group for the headline act, Rockability.

"Massive," Carl said, whistling. "I didn't think you'd have anything like this here."

"River Heights isn't exactly Hick City," Nikki replied, slightly irritated. As if Chicago were the center of the world!

"I guess not, but it's definitely not Chicago." Carl's eyes moved from the interlocking dance platforms to the brilliant light display that sizzled and strobed with the beat.

"That's what's so nice about River Heights. It's in between a big city and a small town," Nikki said defensively.

"If you say so," Carl said, sounding unconvinced.

Nikki tried to concentrate on Tim. He smiled at her as if to say, "Just ignore Carl" and whispered, "Come on, let's dance."

Nikki brightened. "Great!" At last she'd have Tim all to herself.

"What about me?" Carl protested jokingly. "You're not going to leave me here by myself, are you?"

"I'll save the last dance for you," Tim assured him.

Carl shook his head. "Sorry, you're not my type."

"Good! Then find someone to dance with."

"I will," Carl promised, scanning the throng on the dance floor.

Tim reached for Nikki's hand just as the lead singer for the band announced, "We're going to take a ten-minute break. Don't go away now."

"Wouldn't you know?" Nikki said. Things were not starting out very well.

Tim shrugged. "I'll get us something to drink."

"I'll come with you," Nikki said, still holding his hand.

"I'll wait here," Carl said from behind them. "Get me a root beer and some fries, okay?" he added.

Tim slung his arm across Nikki's shoulders and guided her through the throng. "I really hope you don't mind too much that I brought Carl along," he said, once they'd reached the snack bar and were waiting for their order. "But I couldn't let him sit at home by himself. He did come all the way from Chicago just to see me."

Nikki shrugged. "Well, I'd rather have you all to myself, but I guess I can share. It's only for the weekend, right?" Homecoming weekend, she added to herself.

"Right," Tim replied.

Carl caught up with them as they were carrying their soft drinks, fries, and nachos toward a table.

Picking his way through the crowd, Carl suddenly stopped dead in his tracks. Nikki ran into him and sloshed root beer all over the floor.

"Hey, watch out," she said, but Carl wasn't listening. His eyes were glued to the door. "Who is that?" he asked.

Nikki stood on tiptoe and squinted through the darkened interior, past the ever-shifting crowd. Her gaze landed on Brittany Tate. Of course! Who else but Brittany could have struck Carl speechless?

Nikki had to admit that Brittany was a knockout that night. Her long dark hair was pulled to one side and fell past her shoulders in a single shiny braid. As Brittany moved through the crowd, Nikki could see she was dressed in slim-fitting black jeans and a billowy white blouse with a short black leather jacket draped over her shoulders. She was waving to someone in the crowd.

"That's Brittany Tate," Nikki told Carl. "Do you want an introduction?"

"You *know* her?" Carl still looked stunned. "She's gorgeous."

"She's in our class," Tim said.

Carl grinned. "You know, Cooper, River Heights is looking better and better."

Tim waved Brittany over. She lit up at the sight of him—until she spied Nikki and Carl. Nonetheless, she made her way through the crowd. As soon as she reached them, Tim introduced Carl to her.

As if on cue, the band tuned up again. A table became vacant and Tim put their tray down on it.

Carl leaned close to Brittany. "How about a dance?" he suggested.

"Sure." Brittany smiled coyly, pleased by her latest conquest. Tim's friend wasn't so cute as Tim or Jack Reilly, but he wasn't bad looking. And he was obviously interested in *her.* Besides, she still didn't have a date for homecoming.

Some of the college crowd did hang out at Commotion. Brittany had hoped to find a more mature guy, but it wouldn't hurt to be seen with Carl.

As they danced, Carl tried to hold Brittany a little too close, but she managed to keep him at arm's length. She wasn't *that* interested in him. When the song ended, she was able to persuade him to return to the table.

Dipping a tortilla chip in salsa, Brittany looked up and noticed Rick Stratton and Lacey arrive at their table. Rick had filled out a lot over the summer, and Brittany felt a little pang of envy when she noticed how he gazed at Lacey. What exactly was his fascination with that red-haired mouse in lace and ruffles?

Lacey, her arm tucked tightly into Rick's, glanced around the table. She seemed surprised to see Brittany there, and she shot Nikki a what's-going-on look.

Introductions were made quickly, and Lacey pulled up a chair next to Nikki. "This is a new twist," she whispered, nodding toward Brittany.

"I know," Nikki whispered back, shaking her head.

"Come on, let's dance," Brittany said suddenly to Carl. She took his hand and pulled him toward the dance floor, but her eyes were on the far wall, where several boys from Westmoor University were hanging out.

"I don't get it," Lacey said.

"Me, neither." Nikki decided she didn't really care. As long as Brittany entertained Carl, she could have Tim all to herself.

On the dance floor, Brittany kept her arms rigid so that Carl wouldn't get the wrong idea. What a geek! But he looked okay, and he couldn't take his eyes off her.

It was better if the guy played a little hard to get. Well, maybe not so hard as Tim Cooper, Brittany corrected herself. Somewhere there had to be a happy medium: a guy who could interest her and still adore her.

"You're a great dancer," Carl said.

Yuck. Brittany bit back a stinging reply. "I've taken a lot of lessons," she answered. She tried her best to be polite while she searched the room for better prospects. "So you're from Chicago," she said over the thrum of the music. "Tell me about it."

That was all the prodding Carl needed. He geared up and droned on about Chicago as if it were the only city on earth. Brittany barely heard a word. She smiled woodenly and nodded as if she cared, but her gaze kept moving over the ever-changing crowd.

From the corner of her eye, she spied Jack Reilly entering the club. He looked so mature and sophisticated compared to the high-school boys. And he had shown more than a little interest in her at the meeting the other night.

Jack made his way to the snack bar, then turned and looked out over the crowd, checking out the scene.

Unconsciously, Brittany reached up and smoothed her hair.

Jack's gaze finally met Brittany's. He grinned, as if he was amused to see her with

Carl. Brittany's heart skipped a beat and she looked away.

Maybe he'll ask me to dance, Brittany hoped silently, her breath constricting.

"Want something to eat?" Carl asked.

"What?" Brittany asked, startled.

"I asked if you'd like something to eat," Carl repeated.

Since the food was at the snack bar and so was Jack, Brittany suddenly found herself hungry. "Sure," she replied. "I'll go with you." Following Carl, she snaked a trail through the gyrating bodies to the snack bar. While Carl ordered, Brittany cautiously stole a glance at Jack. She moved a few steps closer to Jack, while Carl talked to the waitress.

Jack flashed her another heart-stopping grin, and Brittany felt her temperature rise five degrees. Jack's eyes smoldered.

Brittany swallowed against the lump that had formed in her throat.

Jack sauntered over, his eyes never leaving hers. "Are you with him?" Jack asked, slowly nodding his head toward Carl.

Brittany's mouth felt like cotton. "Why, no. Actually, we just met."

Jack's grin widened. "Then you're still single?"

"Tonight I am," Brittany answered, hoping to give Jack the impression that she had boys lined up to date her.

"Well, so am I," he said, smiling slowly.

Maybe now he'd ask her to dance! Brittany's heart pumped wildly until she glimpsed Carl, who was rejoining them. Oh, no! Not now! She needed a couple more minutes alone with Jack!

"Come on, Brittany," Carl said, balancing a tray of drinks, onion rings, and french fries.

"Yeah, sure." She flicked her eyes back to Jack's and reached up slowly to adjust her braid. "Well, Jack, see you later."

"Probably," he drawled. Was he laughing at her? He held up his glass of soda in a mock salute, and his eyes glinted.

Jack *was* laughing at her! Suddenly irritated, Brittany felt the urge to hurl some horrible insult at him. Who did that guy think he was? With all the aplomb she could muster, Brittany forced a satisfied smile to her lips, tossed her head, and linked her arm through Carl's. At least Carl appreciated her. Jack Reilly could eat his heart out!

From Tim's arms on the dance floor, Nikki had watched Brittany in action. All smiles and knowing glances, Brittany flirted outrageously with both Carl and Jack Reilly.

What was Brittany's game? Nikki wondered, but she decided not to worry about it too much. After all, Brittany *was* giving Nikki and Tim some breathing room, and Carl seemed happy enough.

Nikki and Tim danced silently, wrapped in each other's arms as a slow, sultry song filled the huge club. Nikki rested her head against Tim's chest, hearing his heart beating in steady counterpoint to the music, feeling the soft cotton of his shirt against her cheek.

The song ended and the warm-up band left the stage amid claps and cheers. Commotion was getting even livelier.

"You know," Tim said suddenly after kissing Nikki's forehead, "I hate to break this up, but I've got to go."

"Go?" Nikki repeated, startled. "Where?"

"Home. I promised my mom and dad I'd bring Carl home early." His arms fell to his sides.

Nikki frowned. Carl? "Why?" she asked.

"He said he was up pretty late last night, and he's really tired."

"But Rockability is going to play in fifteen minutes!" Nikki protested. "They're headlining tonight!" What was all this about? Tim was shutting her out again; she could feel it. If he had to go home so early, why hadn't he said anything to her before?

"There's nothing I can do," Tim insisted. "I guess I should have told you when I made the date."

"It would have been nice," Nikki replied, disappointed and growing angry. Now what? Had she done something wrong? Tim started toward the table where Carl was still engrossed with Brittany, but Nikki caught his sleeve. "What's wrong, Tim?" she demanded. "Can't you tell me? You can't go on hiding whatever it is from me forever!"

Tim's lips compressed. "I'm *not* hiding anything," he said angrily, then motioned to his friend. Carl said a hasty goodbye to a startled Brittany.

"So soon?" Lacey protested as Nikki and Tim passed her and Rick. "We just got here!"

"Sorry." Tim's voice was firm. As they headed toward the door, Tim sighed and took Nikki's hand in his. "Please," he begged, "just try to understand, okay?"

"How can I? You won't tell me what's going on," Nikki said, tears clogging her throat.

"Oh, Nikki—" Tim began.

But Nikki didn't want to hear any more of his lies. She shoved her way past him and through the doors. Outside, a fine rain was falling. Puddles had collected on the sidewalk, and the reflected light from the street lamps shimmered against the slick asphalt of the road.

Tim silently helped her into the car. Then Carl, acting as if nothing was wrong, began yammering away about anything that came into his head. Nikki's head started to throb.

By the time Tim pulled into the Masterses' driveway, Nikki had a raging headache and was too upset to wait for Tim to walk her to her house. Throwing open the door, she leapt out and dashed through the puddles to her front door.

"Nikki, wait!" Tim cried, catching her elbow as she reached the porch. "Wait, please!"

Whirling around, Nikki saw Tim's face illuminated by the porch light. His features seemed twisted by some inner torture, and rain slid down his cheeks and throat. He was so handsome, but he looked so tormented. Why?

"Just give me a chance to explain," he begged.

"Explain what?" Nikki demanded. "Explain why you say you love me one minute and act as if you hate me the next?"

"I don't—" he began.

"Why do you detest my car, then?"

Tim's mouth dropped open, but he shut it again quickly.

"What is it, Tim?" Nikki pleaded. "What's the big secret?"

His gray eyes were deep in shadow, and Nikki couldn't read them. Nikki wanted to shake some sense into him, to beg him to love her, but she held on to her pride as she flung the front door open and strode into the house.

Nikki waited in the front hall until she heard Tim's car pull out of the drive. Then she raced upstairs to her room, threw herself onto the bed, and finally gave in to the tears that had been building behind her eyes for the past half-hour.

10

"I'm sorry, Nikki!"

Saturday afternoon, kneeling on the fifty-yard line on the football field, Nikki glanced up from the float she was putting the final touches on. Tim was standing in front of the outstretched paw of the huge papier-mâché Bedford bear. His fists were jammed in the back pockets of his jeans, and he stared down at her with such misery that she felt instant remorse.

Pushing her hair out of her face, Nikki straightened. "You know, when I was younger, my mother told me that just saying you're sorry isn't enough sometimes."

"I know." Tim stared out across the field and let out a long breath that plumed white in the late-afternoon chill. "Look, I guess there is something you should know about me."

Here it comes, finally, Nikki thought.

"I've been trying to hide it from you, but—well, I'm still homesick," he admitted, blushing darkly. "You know, River Heights is a lot different from Chicago. I've lived in a big city all my life, and I made a lot of friends there. Some, like Carl, I've known since grade school. And here"—he motioned to all the students working on the various floats—"it's great and all, but sometimes I still feel like a stranger."

Tim had told Nikki this before, but she hadn't really believed him.

"It's been even worse the last couple of days," Tim went on. "Since Carl's been here, I've missed Chicago a lot more."

Nikki's throat tightened. "And Yvette?"

Tim frowned. "I *don't* miss Yvette. How could I, when I have you?"

Nikki's heart constricted. Tim grabbed her hand, pulled her behind the nine-foot bear, and kissed her hard. Their lips lingered, and Nikki wound her arms around Tim's neck.

"We're still on for the dance tonight, aren't we?" he asked, breaking away and looking into her eyes.

"You never asked me," Nikki said simply.

"I just assumed it was all arranged." His gray eyes turned serious. "What a jerk I was. I just took it for granted that we'd go. I'm sorry. Will you go with me? Please?"

"Oh, Tim!" Nikki smiled up at him, her anger dissolving. "I can't wait!"

Tim grabbed her around the waist and spun her off her feet. Nikki couldn't control the giggles that escaped from her throat. Tim loved her—she could feel it!

"Just promise me one thing," she insisted, laughing as he set her down again. She tried her best to be serious. "If you ever want to talk about anything," she told him, "*anything,* please come to me."

"I will," he whispered. "And there *is* something. Maybe someday soon . . ."

"How about now?" she suggested.

Tim glanced around nervously. "Not here. But later, I promise."

"What's it about?" Nikki asked.

Tim hesitated. "Chicago." His eyes held hers, and Nikki's knees went weak.

"When?" Nikki pressed.

"Later. Right now I just want to concentrate on you." Tim kissed her again, and Nikki tried to ignore her doubts. She and Tim were coming closer together, closer to the truth!

As he held her, Nikki told herself to take things slowly. One step at a time. Because, no matter what, Tim was worth it.

Brittany breezed onto the field and smiled as she watched the float preparations. Inside, the gym looked like a fairyland, draped with blue and white streamers and a huge mirrored ball that hung from the center of the ceiling.

Everything was going according to plan— even her father had helped, by innocently sabotaging the batons for the alumni skit. Just one more thing was left to do. Brittany suddenly spotted the boy she was searching for and waved to him.

Jed Hankins, a sophomore, rose to the bait like a fish to a lure. He hurried past a couple of floats to Brittany's side.

"There have been some last-minute changes for the band, Jed," she told him, batting her lashes. She knew he was barely listening.

Brittany reached into her book bag. "As you know, the band teacher is sick and Marshall will be in charge. Someone just handed me these new instructions for the band. I said I'd find Marshall, but I really don't have time. Would you make sure that

Marshall gets them?" She smiled at him and watched as the poor kid practically melted.

"Yeah, sure," Jed said.

"It's very important," Brittany said. "The halftime show has to go off without a hitch."

"I'll take care of it," Jed vowed, and Brittany knew he would. Silly little fool! He dashed off toward the far end of the field where the band was practicing. Brittany felt as if one more piece of her intricate plan had fallen neatly into place. Now all she had to do was sit back and wait for Nikki Masters's downfall.

She was starting toward one of the better floats, a huge Bedford High bear that would fall in a mock battle with a River Heights High Raider during halftime, when she suddenly spied Miss Have-It-All and Tim wrapped in each other's arms. Brittany's stomach turned.

But she pasted a smile on her face and swept through the grass to them. "How's everything going?" she asked Nikki loudly.

Nikki's blue eyes were positively luminous as she pried herself away from Tim to greet Brittany. "Great."

She blushed and Brittany felt even sicker. "So, everything's on schedule?"

"Mmmm," Nikki replied, looking at Tim.

"Speaking of which"—Tim glanced at his watch and scowled—"I've got to go. I told Carl I'd meet him in the gym. I'll see you tonight, okay?"

Nikki nodded.

Tim's dimples deepened. "Later," he called over his shoulder.

Nikki stared after him for a moment, then swung her gaze back to Brittany. "I've talked to the alumni, and the only things they are still missing are the batons—"

"Right here!" Brittany whipped four silver batons from her huge shoulder bag. "Just don't use them before the actual skit, okay?"

"Can't we even test them?" Nikki asked.

"No. That would foul everything up," Brittany told her. "My dad tested them and they're fine, but he said they'll only work once because they're pressurized or something."

Nikki's brow wrinkled. "Pressurized? How?" She turned over one of the batons.

Brittany's mouth went dry, but she shrugged innocently. "I wish I knew," she lied. "But I'm lousy at all that technical stuff. I think it has something to do with how far the confetti will spew," she babbled on, hoping Nikki would buy her story.

Nikki nodded. "Okay. We'll just have to keep our fingers crossed and hope that they'll work. Now, have you heard from Claire Halliday?"

Brittany shook her head. "No. Why?"

"She's the only person from the alumni skit who hasn't checked in. She's supposed to play the football captain." Nikki glanced around the field, as if she expected Claire to appear out of thin air.

"She'll show up," Brittany predicted, sounding cheery. "And everything will run smoothly."

"I hope so," Nikki said, but she wasn't convinced. At the alumni meeting, Claire had said she'd be back in River Heights early. "I think I'll check with some of the other kids and call her house. Maybe someone's heard from her by now," Nikki said.

"If you think you should," Brittany said. "I wouldn't worry about it."

"It's important," Nikki insisted. "I don't want *anything* to go wrong tonight!" She sighed. "I'll see you later, Brittany."

"Ciao." Brittany waved her fingers, and Nikki took off at a sprint. She dashed into the building and down the one unlocked corridor to where the phones were.

Rounding the corner at a dead run, she collided with Tim's friend Carl.

"Hey, whoa!" he said. "Where's the fire?"

Nikki laughed. Now that she and Tim had cleared the air, she was determined to be nicer to Carl. "I thought you were supposed to meet Tim in the gym," she said.

Carl frowned. "I thought he said the corridor."

"He just went to the gym," Nikki told him.

"Where is it?" Carl asked.

"I'll take you there," Nikki offered, "right after I check something out."

Carl eyed her in surprise. "Your mood sure has improved since last night."

Had it ever! "Yeah, well, I guess I owe you an apology," Nikki said. How could she explain all of this? "You see, uh, Tim and I have been having a little trouble lately."

"So I gathered." Carl's smile slowly disappeared. "I probably didn't help matters by showing up here."

Nikki shook her head. "No! You've been great. Tim needs you. He misses his friends."

Carl raised his eyebrows. "He told you that?"

Nodding, Nikki leaned one shoulder

against the wall. "Yep. He finally explained everything. But it was really hard for him, you know. He doesn't like to talk about some things."

"Can you blame the guy?" Carl asked. "It hasn't been easy for him. But I told him that if only he would confide in a few friends down here about what happened in Chicago, he'd feel lots better."

Nikki's heart nearly missed a beat. What was Carl talking about? Certainly not Tim's homesickness!

"For the longest time," Carl went on, "Tim didn't want anyone to know about the accident. All that guilt, you know."

"Accident?" Nikki repeated, stunned. *What accident?*

"Right." Carl stopped, and his face suddenly lost all its color. "Tim did tell you everything, right?"

Nikki gulped. "Nothing about any accident."

"Oh, gee, look—" Carl rubbed the back of his neck. "I shouldn't be the one to tell." He backed away slightly, looking as if he wanted to take off somewhere.

"You *have* to tell me," Nikki insisted, grabbing Carl's arm.

"Tim would kill me!" Carl protested.

"But you can't just leave me hanging like this," Nikki cried. "Was Tim in some kind of accident or what?" By now she had backed Carl into a corner. "Tell me, please. This is awful."

Carl clamped his mouth shut. He looked at the ceiling, the floor, the walls—anywhere but at Nikki's eyes. Finally he sighed. "I guess you have a right to know."

"Know what?" Nikki's mind was already spinning through all kinds of horrible scenarios. Just what had Tim been hiding?

"He's going to kill me," Carl said again.

"If he doesn't, I *will*," Nikki threatened. "Come on, Carl, *please*. I really care about Tim."

"Okay, okay!" Carl said, throwing up his hands. "But remember, you forced it out of me."

"Just tell me!" Nikki insisted.

Carl squared his shoulders. "It happened just before Tim moved here. When we all found out that he was leaving Chicago, we got together and threw him a going-away bash. Everyone we knew found out about it and showed up, kegs of beer appeared, and the music kept getting louder. Believe me, it started out as just a couple of guys getting together, but before we knew it, things had gotten out of hand. *Way* out of hand!"

"Go on," Nikki whispered.

"Well, Tim's best friend, Alex, insisted on driving a few of us guys home. Alex had had a few beers, and Tim didn't want him to drive anyone anywhere."

Nikki's blood turned cold.

"Well, Alex got mad and said that Tim didn't trust him to drive." Carl's eyes grew dark. "So Alex wouldn't take no for an answer. He had a new silver Camaro, and he wanted to show it off. Anyway, he climbed behind the wheel with Tim beside him, and the rest of us piled into the back. Everything was going fine until Alex just slumped over. He must have passed out. Tim grabbed the wheel, but it was too late. The car veered off the road and crashed into a tree."

Nikki let out a little moan. Tim had been through so much! Tears burned at the back of her eyes.

Carl shuddered a little, and the lines around his mouth deepened.

"And Alex?" Nikki asked softly.

Carl shook his head sadly. Beads of sweat were collecting on his forehead. "He, uh, didn't make it. The rest of us were lucky. We got away with only a few cuts and bruises, but Alex was killed instantly."

"Oh, no!" Nikki whispered, her whole body beginning to tremble.

"Everybody had a rough time getting over it, but Tim took it harder than anyone else. Since the party was for him, and he knew that Alex had been drinking too much, he felt responsible. He's been carrying around this huge load of guilt ever since. He, uh, can't stand flashy cars or wild parties or anything that reminds him of Alex or that night."

Nikki blinked rapidly. No wonder Tim couldn't stand to ride in her car or even look at it! Carl's story explained so much. "I—I didn't know," she said, wishing she'd been more understanding of Tim. But why hadn't he told her? Didn't he trust her?

"Maybe I shouldn't have told you," Carl said, his color beginning to return.

"I'm glad you did," Nikki said. Her heart was breaking for Tim. Why couldn't he have shared this with her? Maybe she could have helped. She would have done so many things differently. "I just wish he had confided in me," she told Carl.

"It's not that easy," Carl replied. "I have trouble talking about it myself." He hesitated. "Listen, I really do have to find Tim," Carl said.

Nikki nodded. "Right."

"I'll catch you later," Carl said. "Probably tonight."

Nikki said goodbye and pointed Carl toward the gym. Her thoughts were no longer on homecoming or dances or floats or alumni skits. All she could think about right then was the incredible burden Tim Cooper was carrying. Somehow, no matter how hard he fought her, she'd help him through this.

She *had* to.

"Nikki!"

Still stunned from the story Carl had just told her, Nikki wandered back outside without calling Claire's house. Nancy Drew, her reddish blond hair streaming behind her, was now racing toward her.

"I've got some bad news," Nancy said breathlessly.

"What is it?" Nikki asked.

"Claire Halliday just called. She's fogged in at the L.A. airport. There's no way she'll get back in time for the alumni skit tonight."

Nikki clapped her palm to her forehead. "Oh, no."

"Wait," Nancy said. "It gets worse. I've

talked to *everyone,* and no one can take Claire's place! All of the alumni, including yours truly, are already in the skit or else they'll be busy with other jobs during the production."

"Great," Nikki murmured, trying to focus on this new problem.

"Can you find a girl to fill in?"

"I'd do it myself," Nikki said, "but I've got to be available if anything goes wrong." She forced herself to try to think of someone who could play Claire's part. Then Nikki heard the sound of familiar laughter drifting over the field.

Brittany Tate! "Come on," Nikki told Nancy. "I know just the person." Brittany loved an audience, and she'd seen the skit twice. She'd be perfect!

Together, Nancy and Nikki ran toward the sound of her laughter and found Brittany talking with Jack Reilly.

This couldn't have worked out better, Nikki thought. Jack was already going to play the head cheerleader in the skit. "Brittany!" she called.

Brittany cast Nikki a perturbed look. "Nikki. What's going on?"

"I— Well, we need your help." After quickly explaining the situation, Nikki added, "We need someone to fill in for Claire. How about you?"

"Me?" Brittany blanched. "Oh, Nikki, I couldn't!" Her mind whirled. She'd made sure that the marching band would get the wrong signals—and then there was the little matter of the shaving cream!

"Come on, Brittany. We're really in a bind," Nancy urged, glancing at Jack.

"Hey, why not?" he asked.

Brittany was tongue-tied for an instant. It *would* be a chance to be with Jack, but—

"Please, Brittany," Nikki pleaded.

Brittany smiled. Nikki Masters was practically down on her knees.

"What about one of your friends?" Nancy asked.

Brittany pretended to mull the situation over. "Kim and Samantha are already riding on another float, and Chris is a cheerleader."

"You know the skit!" Nikki broke in. "You'd be perfect."

"Well . . ." Brittany said.

"Come on. For the good of the school?" Nancy prodded.

"Well . . ." Brittany said again, and glanced at Jack from beneath the fringe of her long lashes.

"It'll be fun," Jack said, squinting against the lowering sun.

"Okay, okay." Brittany gave in, enjoying being the center of so much attention. There was still plenty of time left before the skit for her to fix everything so there'd be no shaving cream squirted. The minute she got Jack alone, she'd warn him not to press the buttons on the batons.

"Well, since that's settled, I guess I'll go get ready," Jack said. His voice rose to a falsetto. "We girls take *hours* getting ourselves together, you know."

"Oh, please." Nancy laughed as Jack dashed across the parking lot.

"Jack!" Brittany called after him wildly. She had to warn him about the batons!

Jack glanced over his shoulder. "Later, Brittany."

Brittany's mouth fell open in dismay. She wasn't going to get to warn him now. She'd have to see him before the skit!

Fans yelled into the crisp September night air that was scented with the smell of popcorn, hot dogs, and peanuts.

Floodlights illuminated the field as the sweaty football players yanked off their helmets and ran to the locker room. The crowd was on its feet, stomping and cheering. At halftime, the scoreboard flashed thirteen to twelve. River Heights had a narrow lead!

Brittany, wearing an ugly, awkward football uniform, was in a panic. She'd put off contacting the drum major, Marshall, assuming she could reach him just before halftime. But now she'd been trying to find him for the last hour. She had to change the signals back so that the band would enter the field at the right time. No one would listen to her. All their orders had to come from that twerp Marshall. Now, as Brittany nervously adjusted her shoulder pads behind the stands, her mind was spinning. There she was, stuck on a float, and she had to come up with Alternate Plan B.

How was she going to warn Jack about the batons so he wouldn't know what she had done? That had been worrying her the last couple of hours, and she still hadn't come up with a good way to do it.

Brittany moaned. What had she gotten herself into? At least she did still have time to warn Jack. Beginning to perspire, she caught a glimpse of that guy — what was his name? — Tim Cooper's friend from Chicago. Carl! That was it! Thank goodness! She'd never seen a poorer excuse for a lifesaver in her life, but she was in a real bind now. "Carl! Over here!" She waved frantically.

Carl's eyes widened at the sight of her. "Brittany?" he asked, taking in her clunky football uniform and the black stuff smeared under her eyes.

"Hi. Uh, listen, I need you to do me a big favor real quick." Brittany flashed him her most dazzling, female-in-distress smile.

He grinned. "Anything."

"Do you have a pen?"

Carl reached into his shirt pocket and produced a felt-tip marker.

"You have to find the drum major of the marching band," she said, "and tell him they're to go back to the timetable for the band. Tell him the band teacher told you."

"Sure," Carl said easily. "Who is the drum major?"

"A tall, brown-haired guy. His name is Marshall Fitzgerald," Brittany told him.

"Oh, great. I've only met about a hundred guys in River Heights who fit that description," Carl said.

Brittany looked at him as if he were crazy. "But he'll be in a band uniform with a tall hat on. He'll be *with* the band. Ask any band member to point him out."

At Carl's blank look, she nearly screamed. Calm down, Brittany told herself. "Look," she said finally, "ask anyone. Everyone knows Marshall."

"Does this mean you'll meet me at the dance later?"

Brittany barely held on to her patience. She could already hear the band tuning up. "Yes," she lied, forcing a sugary smile. "Just make sure you see Marshall!"

"I'll try," Carl promised.

Do more than try, Brittany thought as he hurried off. She wanted to watch Carl, but right then she had something even more important to do. She had to find Jack and tell him about the batons—her time had run out.

"Hey, Brittany! It's showtime," Jack called out to her. He was already on top of the cake float. Dressed in a short cheerleader's skirt and sweater and wearing a blond wig, he looked so silly that Brittany actually giggled.

"Cute," she said, running up to the float.

Jack grinned. "I thought you'd like it. I just hope no one from my fraternity's here," he added as he helped Brittany up.

"Don't worry about it," Brittany said, "you're the cutest cheerleader in River Heights history. Listen, Jack—"

Just then the marching band started to play the River Heights fight song as the float began to roll forward.

"Oh, no! Not now!" Brittany cried in horror. Carl hadn't gotten to Marshall on time!

"Stage fright?" Jack asked.

"No." Brittany glanced around them quickly. "Look, Jack, don't push the buttons on your batons—"

"What?" Jack yelled to make himself heard over the noise.

The crowd in the stands had risen to their feet and was clapping in time to the music. The engines of the trucks pulling the floats roared.

"I said—" But Brittany's voice was drowned out. The float lurched forward, leading the parade onto the field.

Something was wrong—terribly wrong. Nikki watched the scene in amazement from the track in front of the bleachers. The timing was completely off! The floats were coming onto the track from one side of the field, and the band was marching in from the other!

"What's going on?" Tim whispered beside her.

Nikki was so engrossed in the upcoming

disaster that she hadn't even known Tim was there.

"Everything," she moaned.

"Like what?" Tim asked.

"The band's not supposed to be on the field until the alumni float rolls by the stands and the skit is finished!" Nikki told him.

"Is that so bad?" Then Tim took a good look at the action just beyond the field. His face fell.

"There, at least, is a friendly face!" Carl shouted to them from below. He began shoving through the students gathered near the track. His face was red, and sweat dampened his brow. "I've been looking everywhere for some guy named Marshall Fitzsomething!"

"The drum major?" Nikki asked, confused. "Why?"

"Brittany said there was a foul-up. She told me to tell this Marshall to go back to the original timetable. But I couldn't find him."

Nikki's mind raced ahead. The entire halftime show was about to become the biggest mess in the history of River Heights High! "Can you and Carl signal the band to retreat?"

"We can try," Tim offered. "Come on."

The two boys ran to the edge of the field.

They shouted, whistled, and waved wildly to Marshall. The drum major saw Tim waving and frowned.

"Come on, Marshall!" Nikki said, though she knew he couldn't hear her.

Marshall raised his baton, then whistled sharply, swung around, and motioned to the band to stop.

At the same time the alumni float stopped in front of the stands. Nikki held her breath and crossed her fingers. Brittany and Jack played their roles to the hilt, and the crowd behind Nikki roared with laughter.

Brittany, twirling one baton, nearly dropped it. She scrambled, grappling with the silvery rod, and triggered a stream of white foam that squirted all over her surprised face. Sputtering, she lost control of her other baton. It shot foam on several of the other kids in the skit. They shrieked and laughed.

Jack, taking his cue, bravely triggered one of his own batons. Shaving cream covered his face, his clothes, and the top of the "cake."

The audience howled as Jack lost his footing and slid to the edge of the float, dragging Brittany with him and knocking her helmet off. The impact triggered the final baton; it went off, covering the rest of Brittany's face and hair with foam.

Nikki could hardly believe her eyes. The crowd went wild, applauding, laughing, and stomping their feet! Apparently the spectators thought the marching band's antics and the fiasco with the shaving cream were all part of the comedy.

Nikki clapped her hand to her mouth at the sight of a foam-covered Brittany Tate. Her dark hair hung in soapy strands. Her football uniform was wet and sticky, and her face was a brilliant shade of scarlet. Brittany's father must have doctored the batons at her request, Nikki figured. And Brittany had probably had a hand in the band's orders being changed.

There was no doubt about it: Brittany Tate's name was written all over this disaster.

Nikki smiled when she realized that Brittany had been her own victim.

The alumni float continued on its way, as did the other floats. Nikki watched the rest of the ceremony nervously, hoping that Brittany hadn't fouled up anything else.

As the final float, the one with the huge Bedford Bear being felled, drove past, Tim found his way back to Nikki. "What happened?" he asked, his expression dark.

"I think everything went as well as could be expected, considering," Nikki said, swallowing a smile. The skit *had* been hilarious. "No one seemed to realize that there were any problems." She turned to look at the excited spectators. People were still laughing, talking, and cheering.

Tim grinned. "I guess we should be grateful for that." He wrapped his arms around Nikki's waist. "You know," he said, "I think you and I should have a talk."

"Now?" Nikki asked. "You want to talk now?"

"Yes, but not here. Come on." Tim led Nikki away from the noisy crowd, past the school to the tennis courts. A soft breeze kicked up, ruffling Tim's hair, and bringing with it the muffled roar of the fans at the game.

"Carl told me that you know about the accident," he said, pulling her into his arms.

"He didn't mean to—" Nikki began.

"Shh." Tim kissed her softly, and a thrill darted up Nikki's spine. "It's okay. I wanted to tell you, Nikki, but I couldn't."

"Why not?" she asked, gazing up at him.

Tim took a deep breath. "Because when we

left Chicago, I decided to make a fresh start. You know — new school, new friends, no old memories."

"That must have been hard to do," Nikki said slowly. "I know how you must have felt. When I started school this year, I had to face people who knew I'd been accused of murder. I wanted to run and hide, but I couldn't."

"You make me sound like a coward," Tim said.

"You're not a coward," Nikki assured him. "You're just human. And you didn't change your opinion of *me* when you found out about *my* past." Nikki curled her fingers around the collar of his leather jacket and offered him a confident smile. "I won't let anything in your past change my mind about you, either."

"You're a special girl, Nikki Masters," Tim said.

Nikki smiled. "You're pretty special yourself. But you need someone to really talk to. We all do. My friends helped me so much during the murder investigation and afterward. I relied on them a lot, and I hope they would expect the same from me." She thought of Lacey and Robin. What would she do without friends like them to confide in?

Tim sighed and glanced up at the moon,

his eyes taking on a silvery cast. "I just didn't want to blow it with you, that's all."

"You didn't," Nikki said softly.

"What did I do to deserve you, Nikki?" Tim whispered.

"You *don't* deserve me, Cooper," she teased.

Tim laughed. "You're probably right," he admitted, drawing her closer still. His lips, chilled from the cool air, found hers, and Nikki's heart went into overdrive. The night closed in around them, and she was lost in the warmth of Tim.

"Don't ever let go," Tim whispered against her parted lips.

"Never," she promised. And she meant it.

12 ⌇⌇

Jack put one arm across Brittany's shoulders as they rode the float away from the field. "I didn't know this was part of the plan," he said, laughing as his wig, smeared with shaving cream, slid off his head.

"It wasn't!" Brittany hissed angrily.

Jack's smile widened. "Has anyone ever told you how adorable you are with shaving cream on your nose?"

"You planned this," Brittany accused. She couldn't have anyone suspect that she was behind the fiasco.

"Not me." Jack's eyes twinkled, and his arm tightened around her. "But I might have, if I'd known how it would end up."

"Oh!" Mortified, Brittany slid out of his grasp, scrambled off the still-moving float, and ran as fast as her legs would carry her toward the gym. Flinging open the door to the girls' locker room, she dashed inside, her cheeks on fire. Tears stung her eyes. Why had she asked her father to invent those stupid contraptions? Why? She was the laughingstock of the school!

Glimpsing her reflection in a mirror over the sink, she practically shrieked. *Adorable?* Was Jack out of his mind? She looked like last night's mashed potatoes!

Tossing some water over her flaming cheeks, she tried to swallow back her tears. Humiliated, that's what she was. And Jack Reilly was laughing at her, along with all of River Heights! She'd been such a fool!

Stripping off her football jersey, Brittany dropped the wretched shirt on the floor and flung herself onto one of the benches. Her lips trembled, but she forced herself to think. She couldn't let this disaster get her down. She had a reputation to maintain. Somehow she had to blame all of this on Nikki Masters, but how?

With a sigh, Brittany leaned forward, rested her elbows on her knees, and tried to figure a way out of this mess. It would be the talk of the school for weeks, she knew.

"Brittany?"

She froze. Who was in here with her? Someone already looking to poke fun at her?

Cringing inwardly, she opened her eyes. There, half hidden behind a bank of red lockers, was that giraffe, Robin Fisher!

Brittany wanted to die. "What are you doing here?" she demanded, tilting her chin up. Was it her imagination, or were Robin's eyes red? From swimming? Or had she been crying?

"What does it look like?" Robin said with a shrug. "I'm changing."

"But everyone's at the game," Brittany said.

Robin's eyes narrowed. "Not *everyone*," she said, pulling a gorgeous green dress over her trim, athletic body. "You're not."

"I was," Brittany said.

Robin raised her eyebrows. "What happened? Did you fall into a vat of whipped cream?"

Brittany clamped her mouth shut and slowly counted to ten before she trusted her voice. "For your information, I was in the alumni skit, and something went haywire. If you ask me, it was probably Nikki's fault."

"Nikki's?" Robin seemed faintly amused.

"Well, sure. She was student coordinator of the alumni skit," Brittany replied.

"Nikki Masters wouldn't foul up like that. It's more your style, I think!" Robin swiped at her hair, then slung her tote bag over her shoulder. "See ya later, Brittany."

Not if I can help it! Brittany clenched her fists. She hated being ridiculed, especially by Robin Fisher!

Brittany showered, applied fresh makeup, and pulled on a red minidress and a long black jacket. She was going to have to show up at the dance. She would have liked to work a little more on her appearance, but she didn't want to have to confront Nikki Masters or any of the alumni yet—not until she had her story ready.

She grabbed her purse and was on her way out when she heard giggles coming from somewhere nearby. Not now, she prayed silently. Please don't let it be Nikki!

The door burst open, and Samantha Daley and Kim Bishop nearly flew into the locker room. "Oh, there you are!" Kim said. "We've been looking everywhere for you."

Relieved, Brittany forced a wan smile. "You've found me."

"What a great skit!" Samantha raved. "I thought I'd just die!"

"Great?" Brittany screeched. "There was nothing *great* about it!"

"What do you mean? The crowd loved it," Kim told her with a laugh. "And those batons!"

"I have to hand it to Nikki Masters," Samantha drawled, shaking her head. "I don't like that girl much, but that skit was hilarious. And the marching band! What a riot!"

Brittany could hardly believe her ears. Samantha and Kim *liked* the halftime celebration? They thought the skit was *funny?*

"For the first time in years homecoming had some pizzazz," Samantha gushed on. "Even Jeremy Pratt was impressed."

"So who cares what that snob thinks?" Kim demanded.

Samantha's lower lip protruded. "Jeremy's not a snob. He's just a little self-centered, that's all. Anyway, that's not why we were trying to find you."

"Right," Kim said. "Guess who's looking for you?"

Nikki Masters? Mr. Meacham, the principal? Ben Newhouse? Nancy Drew? Brittany gulped. "I, uh, have no idea." She glanced in the mirror and pretended not to be the least bit interested.

"Jack Reilly!" Kim and Samantha cried in unison.

Brittany wanted to sink through the floor. Jack probably hated her now. The joke had no doubt worn off.

"Yeah," Kim went on. "I guess you're pretty lucky Claire Halliday didn't show up." Kim's eyes fairly danced with excitement.

"Otherwise you wouldn't have gotten to work with Jack," Samantha said. "That's who you're going to the dance with, right? The mature guy you've been telling us about?"

Brittany managed to hide her surprise. "Maybe," she said carefully.

"Well, he's looking for you right now," Samantha said. "He said something about wanting to ask you out!"

"He did?" Brittany peered into the mirror, fluffing her hair as if she wasn't the least bit surprised. "Isn't that nice."

"Nice? *Nice?*" Kim repeated. "In case you haven't noticed, Jack Reilly is to die for!"

A pleased smile curved Brittany's lips as she surveyed herself in the mirror. Jack Reilly—a real man, not some high-school boy—was definitely interested in her. "Well, if he's looking for me," Brittany said coyly, "I'd better not disappoint him." The night wasn't turning out so badly after all.

Nikki pressed a soft kiss against Tim's cheek. "So it's settled, right? No more secrets."

Tim pretended to think it over. "Well, maybe just a few."

"Tim Cooper!" Nikki warned, but Tim laughed and squeezed her tighter.

"Come on, Masters. We have a dance to attend." He checked his watch. "We'd better get moving if we're going to meet up with the others."

"The others?" Nikki asked.

"Oh, I forgot to tell you I invited Robin, Calvin, Carl, and Lacey and Rick to go out with us after the dance. I hope that's okay."

Nikki flung her arms around Tim's neck. "Okay? What a terrific idea!"

Tim gave Nikki a tight squeeze. "I'm glad you're happy," he said, his voice growing husky. "I know I am."

Nikki reluctantly pulled away. "I'd better head for the gym to change," she said.

"I'll walk you," Tim said. "Carl said he'd meet me in the guys' locker room. He's got my jacket and tie."

"Does Carl have a date?" Nikki asked.

Tim shook his head. "I don't think so. But he did say something about surprising us with some mystery woman."

"I guess I can wait to find out who she is," Nikki said with a smile, linking her arm in Tim's.

Together they walked through the moon-dusted night toward the gym. In the distance the crowd at the stadium was still roaring. River Heights had just plunged further ahead with another touchdown!

"That's funny," Tim said suddenly.

"What?" Nikki followed Tim's gaze. "Oh, there's Robin now, coming out of the locker room."

Tim frowned. "And there's Calvin. They're taking off for the parking lot. Aren't they going to the dance?"

Nikki looked at him in surprise. "They're supposed to—I thought."

Confused, Nikki watched as Robin slid into Calvin's car. Robin's face seemed unusually pale and puffy in the glare from a nearby streetlight. Had she been crying? What was wrong?

Tim drew Nikki closer to him. "Don't worry," he told her. "They'll catch up with us later at the dance. I have a feeling the two of them want to be alone right now."

Calvin and Robin roared off in the car, and Nikki buried her head in Tim's shoulder. Tim had a point, she knew. But her intuition told her that something was wrong.

"Come on," Tim said. "We're going to have a great time tonight, I promise."

Nikki nodded. She'd talk to Robin later.

Nikki couldn't help feeling a warm glow of happiness. She was with Tim, they were going to the homecoming dance together, and there would never be any secrets between them again.

———————

Now that Brittany has a college guy interested in her, will she be able to handle him? And is Robin and Calvin's romance on the rocks — or out of control? Find out in River Heights #3, *Going Too Far*.